Contents

FOR MY GRANDSON
SHANE MASON

Acknowledgements

A big thank you to my editor, Eilís French, for her careful and sensitive editing. Thanks are also due to Sheila Kiernan of Our Lady of Mercy National School, Kells, who first suggested a link between the *Book of Kells* and Drumshee.

Author's Historical Note

I first got the idea for this book when I was reading a book written about a hundred years ago by a man who climbed Mount Callan, a mountain between Drumshee and the sea. On the mountaintop he found a flagstone, and engraved on it in Ogham (the language of the Celts and early Christians in Ireland) were the words: 'Here lies Conan, the fierce and turbulent.'

Who was Conan? Why was he called fierce and turbulent? How did he die? Who buried him on top of the mountain? All these questions simmered in my head for a few months. Then I saw an aerial photograph of Clogher. Clogher is a small hill about a mile from Drumshee. On top of the hill are the ruins of a church, an old graveyard and a farm. When I looked at the aerial photograph, it showed the outline of an oval boundary wall; and it suddenly flashed into my mind that this might easily have been an ancient monastic settlement. As soon as I thought of that, the whole story of Conan and Columba came to life in my mind. I sat down at the computer and typed:

'I took his body in my arms, and I carried him up to the top of Mount Callan…'

Prologue

I took his body in my arms, and I carried him up to the top of Mount Callan. And I laid him in the shallow grave that I had hollowed out of the stony soil.

Sorcha bent over him and smoothed the dark curls from his face. She took off her purple cloak and laid it over his body.

And then I shovelled the earth over him and hid him forever.

I carried over a heavy flagstone and placed it on the mound, and with my knife I carved on it these words:

Here lies Conan, the fierce and turbulent.

Then I climbed back down the mountain again. Sorcha followed me. She made no sound, but I knew she was weeping. When we reached Liscannor Bay, I turned and looked at her for the last time. But she would not look at me. She shook her fair hair over her face and walked away, leaving me on the sands.

I was not alone, though: the priest was there. He

was looking at me. He stood beside his boat – that small, frail cockleshell made from hazel branches covered with ox-skins. Could a boat like that ever last against the mighty thunder of the Atlantic waves? I shrugged. What did it matter?

'I have come,' I said.

He nodded. I laid my shovel on the golden sand and stepped into the boat. He followed. Neither of us spoke again, and the waves took us and tossed us on the glittering blue of the ocean.

Chapter 1

I have always been cursed. When I was born my mother screamed at the sight of me.

'He's got the mark of the devil on him,' she wept. 'Look at his shoulder! Look at that red mark! That's the imprint of the devil's claw.'

'No, no,' said the priest, when I was brought to the church at Clogher. 'That's the mark of God. We'll christen him Columba, after the saint that established our order here. St Columba will protect him and keep him for himself.'

My mother still wept, though, when they brought me back. 'Take him and put him out under the statue of St Brigid,' she said. 'If the mark is still there in the morning, it will be a sign that he's the devil's child.'

'He may die out there,' said my father.

'It's a summer's night,' said my mother harshly. 'Wrap him warmly.'

'But the mark was still there in the morning, so you're the devil's child, Columba,' finished Conan. He had told me the story again and again – not to tease me, I knew; Conan was good-natured and, on the whole, kind to me. He told the story because he had heard it so often from my mother. I knew it by heart, but I still listened to it. I never wondered how he knew – after all, he had been less than three years old when I was born. I never wondered whether the story was true. I knew it was true. It explained everything.

I often went and sat by the statue of St Brigid, under the old ash tree outside our enclosure. It was peaceful there; the high wall shut out the sounds of my mother's harsh voice calling from our house to my aunt's, the clanging of metal being beaten at the forge, the hiss of hot iron being plunged into water, my father's laughter and words of praise for Conan. I sat there and looked into the strange old face of the stone statue, and wondered why I was so hated.

Conan wasn't hated. Conan was loved. And yet he was my parents' foster-child, and I was their only living child. Even though I was only five years old, this puzzled me. He had come when my elder brother was still alive – they had been babies together; I knew that. My brother had died and Conan had lived. I loved and admired Conan – he could do everything that I couldn't – but I wished my parents loved me as well.

I heard his voice over the wall: 'Look, Father, I'm

strong enough to lift the hammer! Soon I'll be able to hammer out the iron.'

'You will, too.' My father's voice was laughing, but there was pride in it. 'Look at those muscles, Aidan,' he called to my uncle. 'He'll make a great smith, won't he?'

My uncle's voice was low, but I knew what he said because my father answered him.

'You're right; Columba will never be much use. Look at the size of him – six years old, and he has the strength of a newborn kitten. I don't know what I'll do with him. He's useless.'

It was my birthday; I had forgotten that until my father mentioned my age. I was six years old. Conan was eight. He would be nine at Lunasa, at the time of the harvest. There would be a great feast for his birthday, but there was never one for mine. My birth had brought no joy to anyone. My mother could hardly look at me, and my father despised me. I know all that now; but when you are six years old, you don't always realise that there are some things you can't change.

I jumped up; I remember the smell of the meadowsweet under my feet as I ran around the high circular wall of the enclosure and in through the gate. The three houses – ours, my uncle and aunt's and my grandparents' – were shining gold where the new thatch reflected the hot June sun. I ran as fast as my small, thin legs would carry me across the grass of the enclosure, over to the forge near the north wall.

'I'm strong, too,' I gasped – running always left me breathless. 'I'm as strong as Conan. Look at my muscles!'

I held up my puny arm, clenching my fist the way Conan did, and tried to make the little knobs of muscle stand out.

My father began to laugh; but then his face darkened. The short sleeve of my brown wool tunic had fallen back when I lifted my arm, and the red birthmark on my shoulder – the mark of the devil's claw – stood out.

'Get off to your mother,' he said roughly.

My eyes filled with tears – I know because I remember that, when I looked at my mother, she seemed to blur and shift. When I blinked the tears away she was gone; she had gone back into the house and shut the door. I turned away.

I went back through the gate and out to the stone shed where our dog had her puppies. I bent down and tried to pick out one of them – I liked the warm, soft feel of his silky fur – but his mother snarled at me, so I put him back. I walked away; but then I returned and snatched him up again, ignoring the mother's warning growl. I liked this puppy best of all. He was smaller and thinner than his brothers and sisters, and his mother didn't like him as much. I tucked him under my arm and went back to the statue of St Brigid in her little wedge-shaped house of stone.

'Please, St Brigid, could you get rid of that mark from my shoulder?' I whispered.

St Brigid stared back at me with her stone-blind eyes.

'Go on, St Brigid – you could do it if you tried…'

Still she stared at me. I fixed my eyes on the red mark on my shoulder. There was no change; it grew no smaller.

'I don't care,' I said aloud, blinking my tears away. 'I don't care. I've got this puppy all for my own. He's my puppy.'

'No, he's not,' said Conan's voice. 'That puppy's going to be sold. The only one we're going to keep is the one I like, the white one with the patch over one eye. I'm going to call him Patch.'

'No, we're going to keep this one,' I said obstinately. 'Father said so.'

'I bet he didn't,' said Conan. He knew I was lying, of course. I would never have had the courage to ask;

and, even if I had, I would have been refused. I was old enough to know that.

Conan turned away, but then turned back. 'I suppose you might be allowed to keep him because he's so small,' he said. 'What's his name?'

I thought for a moment. It was obvious that a puppy that was going to be kept would have a name.

'Devil,' I said. I hugged the puppy. 'You're the devil's child,' I whispered to him. 'I'm not going to let you go back to your horrible old mother. She lets all the other puppies bully you.'

I remember that I kept the puppy with me all day. When I was called in for my dinner, I put him back with his mother for a while; but I snatched a lump of meat from the table on the way out, and lifted him from his bed and fed it to him piece by piece.

No one had ever loved me the way that puppy did. He never ran away to play with his brothers and sisters, who were staggering around the yard; he always ran straight to me and snuggled against me, with his little tail wagging and his brown eyes full of love.

It didn't last, of course. It couldn't last. Things never go well for a devil's child. One by one the puppies went to new homes – everyone wanted one, as our dog was famous for herding – until only

Conan's puppy Patch, a bold, cheeky little bully, and my little Devil were left.

And then they came: Jarlath the leather-worker from Clogher, his quiet, smiling wife Dervilla, and their little foster-daughter Sorcha. They wanted a puppy. Patch was the one that caught their eye. I hugged Devil to me. They didn't want him. I could keep him for ever and ever.

'You can't have that one,' said my father, picking up Patch. 'The young lad' – he pointed to Conan – 'has a mind to train that one. I wouldn't like to take it away from him now.'

'No, surely, surely,' said Jarlath, his eyes going to me. 'But what about the other pup? Columba seems to have a fancy for him.'

'That's nothing – just a thing of the moment. He's just a child; he'll forget him tomorrow,' said my father roughly. 'No, he's not up to training a dog. He'll ruin him.'

'Very well, then; we'll have the small one. I suppose he'll grow. What do you think, Dervilla?'

Dervilla lifted the puppy gently from my arms and felt his ribs. 'He'll grow,' she said, handing him to her husband. 'He just needs a bit of feeding up, that's all.'

'He's not worth a cartload of turf, though,' said Jarlath. 'I'll give you half a cartload for him.'

'Done!' said my father.

'No!' I screamed. 'No, you can't take him! He's mine. He'll die without me. He loves me. He loves me more than anyone else in the world.'

'We'd better not take him,' said Jarlath. Even though the tears blinded my eyes, I could hear the kind note in his voice, and I knew that he was looking at me with his gentle brown eyes. I blinked away the tears and looked back at him. A small whisper of hope was rising inside me.

'Take him or take him not, whatever you wish,' said my father harshly. 'I'll drown him in the rainwater barrel if you don't want him. Columba can do it for me; he's strong enough for that, I suppose.'

He would do it, too; I knew that. With his unpleasant laugh ringing in my ears, I held out the puppy to Jarlath. I could say nothing; my throat was swollen into a hard lump.

He took the puppy gently and knelt down beside me. 'Do you know where Clogher is?' he asked.

I nodded. I knew Clogher. It was a settlement of monks, each one in his small round stone house, grouped around the church and the bell-tower – 'clogher' was the old word for 'bell'. Jarlath's farm was beside the settlement.

'Well,' he went on, 'I've got a little girl there' – he

smiled at Sorcha, who came over and put her hand confidently in his – 'and this little girl has no playmate. What if you come over to play with her today, so the puppy will be happy to come with us? And then you can run over to us, any day when your father doesn't need you, and play with Sorcha and the puppy. You'll like that, won't you, Sorcha?'

Sorcha nodded. She put her finger shyly in her mouth, but then she took it out and smiled at me. She was a little older than me and she had just lost her front teeth; when she smiled she showed all the gaps, but I had never seen a smile so beautiful. She had corn-coloured hair braided into two plaits, and her eyes were the blue of a summer sky.

'What's the puppy's name?' she asked.

I opened my mouth and then shut it again. I didn't want to say that his name was Devil. I was sorry I had called him that. He was such a sweet puppy; he deserved a name that would bring him good luck.

'You give him a name,' I said, looking into those huge blue eyes.

'We'll call him Honey,' she said decisively. 'He has honey-coloured fur.'

My heart warmed at that word 'we'. I was still going to have a share in the puppy.

'Yes,' I said. 'We'll call him Honey.'

'It's a good name for him because he's sweet,' said Sorcha confidently.

Jarlath put the puppy back into my arms, and lifted us both up and placed us in the cart beside Dervilla. She put her arm around me and gave me a brief hug. Then Jarlath swung Sorcha up, making her shriek with laughter and pretended fear; she snuggled in on the other side of me, leaning across my lap to stroke the puppy.

'I'll give the lad his dinner, and then he'll be able to run back home to you,' Dervilla said to my father. 'Sure, it's only a step from here to Clogher.'

'Keep him as long as you like,' said my father curtly. 'He's no use here, that's one sure thing.'

I looked back as the cart went down the lane. My father was still there, but he wasn't watching after me; his arm was around Conan's shoulders and he was bending down to talk to him. The sound of his laugh echoed in my ears as we went around the corner.

Chapter 2

After that, my life got better. My father didn't care how much I was missing from Drumshee, and my mother's face only darkened when I came near to her. Every morning I herded the cows to their new pasture, and then my work was done for the day. I was never allowed near the forge; that was for Conan. As soon as I could escape, I would be off down the lane and running along the road towards Clogher.

Sorcha would be on the lookout for me. 'Here he is!' she would shout as soon as she saw me.

'Here he is,' Jarlath would call.

'Here he is,' often came from one of the monks on his way to ring the bell in the belltower.

And then Sorcha would be running to meet me, and Dervilla would be there with a drink of buttermilk and an oat-cake, and Jarlath would want me to help him trim a piece of leather in his workshop, and Honey, that sweet-natured, gentle dog, would wag his tail. Even the birds in the trees seemed glad that I was there.

17

Sorcha had lessons from Father Brendan in the monks' enclosure, and it seemed only natural that I should join her. Father Brendan taught us both to read and write and praised the way I handled the quill. He took us into the scriptorium, where the monks copied the sacred gospel books and books of psalms. He often talked to me about St Columba, for whom I was named, and how he had copied so many books so beautifully. He told me the story of how, two hundred years ago, St Columba copied one book that didn't belong to him; this book was so valued that his action caused a great war.

'Many men were killed on both sides,' Father Brendan said solemnly. 'Columba felt so guilty about all those deaths that he decided to punish himself by leaving Ireland, so he sailed away across the sea to the island of Iona, near the country they call Scotland, and set up another community of monks there. Many monks have crossed to Iona since then; perhaps one day I, too, will go there again.' And then Father Brendan would gaze out to the northwest, his large grey eyes narrowed as if he were trying to pierce the clouds and see that faraway island.

I loved to listen to those stories, and I practised and practised to make my copying as good as St Columba's. Father Brendan often called other monks to look at how well-shaped my letters were. He even allowed me to copy a few words into the manuscript he was working on. When it came to writing, it didn't matter that I had weak hands and narrow wrists. Conan had never learned to read and write, and that gave me a good feeling – at least I was better than he in one thing!

I made myself a little scriptorium, just like the monks had at Clogher, in the underground room at Drumshee. It was a small room, deep under the earth in the centre of the enclosure. I had heard that, in the old days, people had used it for storage and as a hiding-place when enemies came, but no one went near it any more; I had it all for myself. I found a goose quill from one of my uncle Aidan's geese for a pen, and I used to make myself inks – black from soot, purple from blackberries, red from raspberries, blue from the woad herb that my mother grew, yellow from boiled onion-skins. Dervilla gave me some white of egg to thicken my inks, and Jarlath gave me all the odd bits of leather trimmed from the sheets of vellum that he used for the monks' books. Often Sorcha used to join me there, and I would make tiny books for her – some about the many wildflowers that grew in the fields of Drumshee, some about Honey, our favourite dog. I signed each of the little books with a drawing of a dove; Father Brendan had taught me that 'Columba' meant 'dove' in Latin, and that it was used as a symbol for St Columba.

Sorcha helped me to make little clay pots for the inks, out of the mud from around the well. We hollowed out the lumps of clay with our small thumbs, dried them in the sun, whitewashed them with lime and then filled them with the differently coloured inks. Before the pots were dry, I lettered the colour of the ink onto each of them; and under the word I drew the dove, my special symbol. It was the first time I had had anything I could truly call my own.

One day Sorcha and I were in our underground room when I heard my father shout, 'Columba! Where's that boy?'

I came out of the dimness of the underground chamber, blinking like a little owl.

'Hurry up, lad,' said my father impatiently. 'I want you to take that calf up to Diarmuid of Drumevin — he's bought it from me. Take good care of it; someone told me there was a wolf seen up near the border.' The border was the high bank, beyond Drumevin, that separated the kingdom of Corcomroe from that of Thomond.

'Can Sorcha come too?' I asked.

My father beamed as she appeared behind me. Like everyone else, he loved Sorcha. The only time he could stand having me around was when she was with me. 'Yes, you go along with him, sweetheart; make sure the big bad wolf doesn't eat him.'

Conan laughed and Sorcha giggled. I scowled. I hated being made a fool of, but I didn't dare say anything. Silently I took the stick in my hand and drove the calf down the lane. He was a bit nervous at being separated from his mother and the rest of the herd, but Sorcha walked beside him, stroking his soft neck and talking to him. By the time we reached Drumevin I had lost my ill temper and we were walking hand in hand, enjoying the day out together and the fine late-August weather.

Diarmuid of Drumevin was a courteous man. He praised our handling of the calf, who had arrived relaxed and calm. 'You're a great help to your father,' he said to me.

Mary, his wife, came out with some ice-cold buttermilk and a honey-cake for each of us. 'Be careful on your way home,' she said to us. 'There are some men out hunting down a she-wolf.'

'Let's go and see if we can find the wolf,' I said to Sorcha as we made our way out of Diarmuid's farm.

'I'm a bit scared of wolves,' confessed Sorcha.

'I'm not,' I boasted. In my mind I could hear my father's gibe, and I was determined to show him – and show Sorcha – that I was no coward. 'Come on,' I said aloud, taking her hand firmly in my own. 'Wolves don't touch people; they only eat cattle. Let's just go a bit nearer the border.'

So we climbed the hill of Knockalunkard and stood looking down. The border was immense. It stretched for miles towards Mount Callan on one side and towards Lough Inchiquin on the other, and on its far side was the kingdom of Thomond. It was a huge bank, six times the height of a man, and on top of it a thick hedge of quickthorn was planted. Neither man nor beast could get through that hedge. The men of Corcomroe had planted it many hundreds of years ago, to keep our small kingdom safe from attack by the mighty kingdom of Thomond.

We gazed to the west, towards the blue mountains of that faraway land; and as we watched we saw men riding towards the bank, on our side of the border. They were mounted on horses, and each of them carried a spear.

'It's the wolf-hunt,' I said. I was half thrilled and half revolted; I didn't want the wolf to be killed, but

I was excited at the thought of the chase.

'Look!' cried Sorcha, her voice shrill with excitement.

A large grey wolf was running along beside the boundary bank. She didn't seem to be trying to escape from the men chasing her; she just ran steadily, desperately, along the side of the huge bank. And then, suddenly, she disappeared.

'She's gone into the bank; she must have a den there,' said Sorcha.

'The men don't know where she's gone,' I said. 'They don't know where to look.'

'Don't tell –' Sorcha began; then she gave an excited scream. 'Look, there she is – and her cubs!'

'Where –' I began; and then I saw her too. The wolf had gone into the bank, but she hadn't come out on our side, in Corcomroe; she had gone right through the bank – which was at least thirty paces wide – and come out on the Thomond side. She was running across a field in Thomond, with three cubs by her side, and as we watched she disappeared into a patch of trees. She was safe; and so were her cubs.

Sorcha and I watched for about ten minutes while the huntsmen went up and down the bank looking for her. None of them knew what we did: there was an underground passage through the boundary bank, leading out into the kingdom of Thomond. They didn't even see the place where the wolf had gone into the bank; but, now that I knew where it was, I could see it clearly, between a small round gorse bush and a fine ash tree.

Eventually the men tired of riding up and down by the boundary bank and turned their horses' heads towards home. When they had gone, I turned to Sorcha. Her eyes were shining with excitement and her cheeks were pink.

'Let's go down,' she said. It wasn't the first time she had read my thoughts. 'Let's see where she went through. Maybe we could go, too. Maybe we could peep into Thomond.'

Not giving ourselves time to think, we ran down the hill and across the fields to the boundary bank. I looked around carefully. No one was near.

'Keep down,' I ordered. 'Don't let anyone see us. Just creep along.'

I don't know about Sorcha's, but my heart was beating very fast. When we came to the ash tree, I was almost hoping that the wolf's hole would be too small for us – that the great adventure would end there, and we would have to turn around and go back to the tranquillity of Clogher and Jarlath's gentle voice.

We found the hole easily enough. I was surprised that the horsemen hadn't seen it; but then, they were high up and we were low, nearer the ground.

'She had her cubs here for a while,' whispered Sorcha.

There were several pieces of gnawed bone lying around. It looked as if the mother wolf had fed her family well; they had seemed to be strong, well-grown cubs when they scampered after her across the fields of Thomond.

'How did she get through?' I whispered back.

For a moment it looked as if there was only solid rock in front of us; but then, as our eyes got used to the dim light, I saw that this was an enormous boulder, and beside it ran a well-worn passage. The wolf was not a wolf of Corcomroe, nor a wolf of Thomond; she belonged to neither kingdom, but hunted on both sides of the borderland.

'Shall we go through?' I whispered, and Sorcha nodded.

I led the way, hoping she didn't know how terrified I was. I tried to count the paces as I went. I had lost all sense of direction, and at first I didn't know whether we were just going along the bank, or going through it; after a few minutes, though, the light grew stronger and I knew that we were coming to the other side of the bank.

'It's Thomond,' I whispered a minute later.

'It looks the same as Corcomroe, doesn't it?' said Sorcha, peering over my shoulder.

'Of course it's the same,' I said, but I knew what she meant: somehow I had expected it to be different.

'There's a man over there!' whispered Sorcha, grabbing my arm.

I followed her pointing finger and saw a man's head turn in our direction – our voices must have been louder than we had realised. A blind panic came over me. I didn't know what the men of Thomond would do if they caught a boy and girl from Corcomroe on their land. Hurriedly I turned and pushed my way back down the passageway, feeling Sorcha grab at my tunic and hold on firmly. As soon as we were out on the Corcomroe side, we began to run as fast as we could.

When we reached the road to Drumshee, we slowed down. 'Never tell anyone about this, Sorcha,' I warned. 'I'd get into terrible trouble if anyone knew we went into Thomond. My father would beat me – he might even kill me. Promise you'll never tell anyone.'

'I promise,' said Sorcha. She was wide-eyed and

frightened, though she was quite safe: neither Jarlath nor Dervilla would ever have laid a hand on her, no matter what she did. 'I don't ever want to go there again,' she added.

'We won't,' I said thankfully.

There was no temptation to go back, anyway. We had work to do: Sorcha learned spinning and stitching and weaving from Dervilla; I learned from Jarlath how to turn ox-hides into leather, how to make the softest vellum for the monks' books from the skins of calves. And then we had Honey to play with, writing to practise, books to make, games to play in the meadow hay. Life was too full for us to bother with putting ourselves in danger by going into the kingdom of Thomond.

# Chapter 3

The first cloud over our happiness came when I was eleven years old. Sorcha was twelve then. I had been busy all morning, helping Jarlath by lifting the big ox-skins from their bath of oak tannin and pegging them onto the fence to dry, and I was tired – I still had little strength; so I was lying down by a haystack, watching the swallows congregate on the branches of the big oak tree in the hedgerow. Sorcha was lying beside me.

'I love Jarlath and Dervilla,' she said softly.

I stroked Honey. He had grown into a fine-looking dog, as big as his brother Patch; but Honey had a gentle, quiet nature – unlike Patch, who was the victor in every dogfight for miles around.

'They're very nice,' I agreed. I didn't want to say I loved them too – I didn't think that sounded manly; it wasn't the sort of thing Conan would say, and at that time in my life I admired Conan with an uncritical devotion. But I did love Jarlath and Dervilla, with all my heart and soul.

'I never want to leave them,' Sorcha went on.

'Why should you?' I asked, tickling Honey's nose with a long stem of the flowering grass.

'I'll have to go in a year or two,' said Sorcha. 'My fosterage will end then.'

I looked at her in shock. I had forgotten that she was only the foster-child of Jarlath and Dervilla. 'Why do you have to go so soon?' I demanded. 'There's no talk of Conan going back to his parents, and he's years older than you – he's fourteen now.'

'That's different,' said Sorcha sadly. 'He's a boy. Girls finish their fosterage at thirteen or fourteen; Conan won't finish his until he's seventeen or eighteen. In any case . . .' She hesitated, then went on, her eyes fixed on me, 'I've heard talk that your father wants to keep Conan, to make him a partner in the forge. He may never go back to his own parents.'

I had heard that rumour, too, but I didn't want to think about it. I didn't want to wonder what was going to happen to me. My uncle Aidan, who ran the farm at Drumshee, had three fine sons of his own; they would be all that the farm would need. The forge was different – my father needed help there; but Conan gave all that was needed. If my father didn't teach me the skills of a blacksmith soon, there would be no place for me at Drumshee.

I pushed my problem to the back of my mind and

turned back to Sorcha's. 'Will you have to go back to Moughna, then?' I asked. Moughna was a stretch of moorland near Mount Callan, and I knew Sorcha's parents lived there.

Sorcha shook her head. 'No; I'm to be married,' she said. 'My parents were over here on Sunday, and they were discussing it with Jarlath and Dervilla – I was sent out, but I listened at the door. They're going to start looking for a good husband for me.'

The sun moved a little, coming out from behind the trees, and a great beam of sunshine from the west lit up Sorcha's face. I looked at her corn-coloured plaits, her pink cheeks and her blue eyes, and it was as if the beam of sunshine lit up my mind as well.

'I'll marry you,' I said eagerly. 'We'll build a little house just near here, and Honey can go back and forth between the two houses.'

Sorcha laughed. She was much more grown-up than I was.

'You're too young,' she said. 'I need someone older than me for a husband. Anyway, he'll have to have an honour-price of at least seven *sét*s. I heard my parents say that. You see, my father has an honour-price of seven *sét*s, so it would be a disgrace to him if I married a man whose honour-price was lower.'

I thought about that. I had never listened much to

talk about honour-prices — although I knew that older people thought about them a lot, as your honour-price gave you your place in society — but I knew that seven *sét*s was the honour-price of a wheelwright; Conor the wheelwright had told me that when he came to bring a new wheel for Jarlath's cart. Of course — Sorcha's father was a wheelwright. Then I remembered what else Conor had said: 'That's the same as the honour-price of a blacksmith.'

I turned eagerly to Sorcha. 'I could marry you if I were a blacksmith,' I said.

She laughed again. It was a gentle laugh — she was always kind — but it was the laugh of an older sister, or even a mother.

'Yes, you could,' she said. That was all. She didn't say — but I knew the truth myself — she didn't say: *You'll never be a blacksmith. You're not big enough, not strong enough. Your father doesn't want you.*

* * *

It must have been at least a year after that when Conan came to Clogher. Jarlath was making a fine leather harness for the Abbot of Clogher's horse, and he had sent me to my father with drawings of the iron bit and the pendants; but when they were made, Conan brought them back himself. Thinking over it now, I know why he came. He had the whole thing worked out in his mind. He had heard about Sorcha. Perhaps my father had put the idea into his head.

He was wearing a new tunic when he came up the hill. It was saffron-yellow and made from the finest linen; my father had got it for him on his sixteenth birthday. His skin never lost its summer tan, and his cheeks glowed. His lips were as red as a girl's, and the rich colour of the tunic set off the black of his curls and the dark brown of his eyes. Although he was only sixteen, his shoulders and chest, developed by all the work at the forge, were bigger than those of most men. He ignored me. He ignored Jarlath. He went straight up to Sorcha.

'Sorcha,' he said. 'Why didn't Columba tell me that you had grown to be such a beauty?'

And she was. Barely fourteen, she had grown to her full height, and her face and figure were those of a woman. Her corn-coloured hair was thicker and richer than ever, and her eyes were the colour of the harebells in the fields in August.

She gave him her hand – and she did not take it back. They stood there, seeing no one else, gazing into each other's eyes. I was sick with jealousy. I was only a boy, only twelve years old, but Sorcha was everything to me. I remember thinking: He's going to take this away from me, too. *He has taken my father and my mother for his own, he has taken my rightful place at the forge, he has robbed me of the means to be Sorcha's husband, and now he is going to take Sorcha for himself…* It was strange, this sudden jealousy, because I loved and admired Conan – he was the only one at Drumshee ever to throw me a kind word.

'So,' said Jarlath dryly, his voice breaking through the mist of my fears and jealousies, 'you've brought the harness-bits, have you?'

With an effort Conan took his eyes from Sorcha. 'Here they are,' he said, delving in his leather satchel and pulling out the iron bit and pendants. He put them in Jarlath's hands. 'See if they're right,' he said. 'I'll wait while you sew them to the leather. If they need any alterations, I can take them back with me.'

Then he turned back to Sorcha, and he smiled. No one could smile like Conan; his whole face lit up as if the sun had suddenly come out. No wonder my mother and father loved him so much.

'Sorcha,' he said, 'let's go and look at the belltower. I hear its bell every day – but, believe it or not, even though I only live a couple of miles away, I've never been close to it. It looks so big! It's like one of your father's needles – a giant needle. It looks as if it could pierce the sky!'

Sorcha laughed. She put her hand in his again; and gaily and happily, without a backward glance, they went off together towards the monks' enclosure.

'Come and help me, Columba,' said Jarlath gently. I went with him. I had never felt as small, as puny, as insignificant as I did in that moment.

The harness-bits were perfect; I had known they would be. Conan was good at his work. The joins were invisible; the rings were perfectly rounded. Jarlath took up the harness that we had made and handed it to me.

'Go on,' he said. 'You do it. Most of this is your work, and I've told the Lord Abbot so. For a boy of your age, you're a great leather-worker. You have a good eye and a steady hand. You would be wasted as a blacksmith.'

I have said that he was kind, always kind, but that day his kindness was wasted on me. I took up my needle and the grass-thin, supple strips of leather that I had softened by drawing them again and again through my clenched teeth. I stitched the leather harness to the shining iron bits, and then I went to the door and looked out. I could see the belltower – its tiny windows, its door set high above a man's reach to keep out intruders – but I couldn't see Conan and Sorcha. They had hidden themselves

34

from view around the back of the tower.

'Have you ever thought of the future?' said Jarlath, behind me. 'Have you thought about what you might do when you're a man?'

I turned to look at him, but my eyes were dazzled by the sun and I couldn't see him.

'Your father believes you might not be quite right for the forge business,' his gentle voice went on. 'I wondered whether you would think of being a leather-worker. I have no child of my own, and Sorcha will leave us shortly – her parents want her to go back home for a few months before they arrange a marriage for her. Dervilla and I would like you to be our foster-son. Then the leather-making business will be yours when I am gone.'

Was ever such an offer made to an unloved boy? And yet I didn't want it. I remembered a lesson with the monks only a few months before, just after Sorcha had told me that she was to be married; she had cross-questioned Father Brendan about honour-prices. I remembered her voice: 'What's the honour-price of a blacksmith, Father?'

And the priest's reply: 'The honour-price of a blacksmith is seven *sét*s.'

'And what's the honour-price of a leather-worker, Father?' I had asked.

'The honour-price of a leather-worker is one *sét*,' Father Brendan had answered.

I had been angry about that. It didn't seem right: Jarlath's work was just as skilled, just as useful as the work my father and Conan did. Why should he have a lower place in society than they had? I had lost interest in honour-prices then.

But now I remembered. If I became a leather-worker, I would have an honour-price of only one *sét*. I would be low in the ranks of society – far lower than Sorcha's parents. There would be no hope that Sorcha would marry me when I was old enough. Even if I grew tall and strong, even if my white-blond hair turned black and my pale-blue eyes darkened; even then, Sorcha would never marry me.

Chapter 4

Another year went by. Sorcha went back to her parents in Moughna. I wondered whether she was happy there. She had spoken of the place a little before, of how she hated the flat, desolate moorland; but she had also spoken of Mount Callan, that mighty mountain that reared its blue shadow to the south. Sorcha loved Mount Callan. And now someone else loved it too.

'You've never been up Mount Callan, Columba, have you?' said Conan one day, punching me boisterously on the arm. He knew I hadn't. It was too far to walk and I, unlike him, had no pony of my own; and who would take me there? He knew that, but he had to talk about it; the joyful feelings that were bubbling inside him were too strong for silence.

'It's the best place in the world,' he went on. 'Sorcha and I went up there last Sunday. We climbed right to the top, and we stood there and looked down at the ocean. The wind was in our faces, and the waves on the ocean were white with foam – it looked as if a herd of wild white horses were tossing

37

their manes down there. It's — it's my place! I felt as if I never wanted to come down to the flat land again.'

I said nothing, but I could see the image, as vivid as one of the little pictures the monks painted on the pages of the sacred books. Everything would be blue and white, and Sorcha's corn-coloured hair would be blowing in the breeze…

'Are you going again this Sunday?' I asked. I wondered whether he would take me — and whether I really wanted to go; whether I wanted to see him and Sorcha together. I was relieved and disappointed at the same time when he said, 'No, this Sunday I'm going to the fair at Coad.'

And then, carelessly kind as he usually was to me, he added, 'You can come too. Jarlath won't mind. I'll buy you a new cloak; that one will be too thin for the winter.'

I wondered where he would get the silver for that. I didn't know whether my father paid him, and I dared not ask. And yet Conan always had silver, always had new clothes — a splendid fur-lined cloak, a silver brooch inlaid with red stones . . . Where did he get the means to pay for all of this? Was it just because I knew how much this finery would dazzle Sorcha's eyes that these questions seemed to come to my mind, and not to anyone else's?

At this time I was still going to Clogher every day. I still worked with Jarlath, but we had said no more about me becoming his foster-son. The place seemed lonely now. Honey missed Sorcha; we all missed her. The sun seemed to have gone out of our lives, and the days were dark.

'You could become a monk, you know, if you don't fancy being a leather-worker,' Jarlath said one day. 'Father Brendan's been talking to me about it. He says you would make a good priest – you have a fine hand at copying, and you can read and write well. He says he can teach you Latin if you start coming for lessons again. He mentioned it to your father too, and your father said you could do what you liked. Would you like to become a priest?'

I shook my head silently and went on scraping the skins. For a moment I half-considered the idea, but then I put it from my head – though I did return to my lessons with Father Brendan, and he began to teach me Latin.

That Sunday morning Conan and I went to the fair in Coad. It was Lunasa, Conan's seventeenth birthday, and my father and mother had planned a feast for that evening. Jarlath and Dervilla were invited; so were Sorcha and her parents; Conan's own parents would come from faraway Fanore, by the sea. It would be a great occasion.

'Do you know what's going to happen tonight?' asked Conan, as we walked together along the muddy track to Coad.

I shook my head. All I could think of was that I would see Sorcha again. I hoped she would think me older-looking, less of a child. I had begun to grow fast, both in strength and in height, during the past few months.

'Father' – that was what he always called my father, his foster-father – 'Father is going to announce the betrothal. He and my own father have got together the bride-price.' He turned to look at me. His cheeks were flushed and his eyes were sparkling. 'I'm going to marry Sorcha,' he said.

I knew it already, of course; but still, my heart thudded and my cheeks reddened. There was no hope for me now. She would never look at me while she had Conan. For a moment I wished that he were dead, that he would fall into the fire at the forge and be burned to death. But then my rage cleared and I looked at him standing there: my brother, my hero. I couldn't wish any harm to him; I loved him too much. It's difficult for me, writing this so many years later, to remember all the confusions in the mind of a fourteen-year-old, but I know these two things were true: I loved Conan, and I was jealous of him.

'Yes,' I said dully. 'I guessed that.'

And, yet, oddly enough, I'd never had such a good day as I had at Coad Fair that Sunday. The fairgrounds were full of stallholders bartering pots, leather buckets, silver brooches, knives, linen tunics and sweet honey-cakes. Conan was a great companion – amusing, kind and encouraging. He seemed much older, these days; when we were younger he had often teased me, but that was gone now. Now I was just a younger brother of whom he was both fond and proud. Now I see how he liked to have a hero-worshipper by his side; but then I just basked in his kindness and closed my eyes to everything else.

'How many honey-cakes could you eat?' asked Conan.

'Try me,' I boasted. I swallowed a dozen cakes before I had to stop; quite a crowd had gathered by then, and everyone was laughing and cheering me on as Conan fed me cake after cake. I was always hungry these days. I knew it had to do with the way I had begun to grow and fill out. From time to time, I remembered how Dervilla had predicted that Honey would grow, and what a fine dog he had become.

Perhaps I was like Honey; perhaps I would be a fine man eventually.

Conan had some sharp iron spears to sell, and I had a leather satchel that I had made from strips of plaited leather. They had been waste strips, and when I showed my work to Jarlath, he – generous as always – had told me that I could sell it or barter it at the fair. Eventually I managed to exchange it for a small silver pin, and I was very pleased with myself. I looked around for Conan; I would use the silver pin on the new cloak he had promised to buy for me.

Conan was at the far side of the fairground, near the spot where the horse-racing had taken place, in the middle of a crowd of rough-looking men. I stared at them. I had seen the men earlier selling fish, though they hadn't spent long at it; they'd seemed to have very few fish to sell. Now they were looking at Conan's spears and talking eagerly. He was listening intently and nodding from time to time.

'Who are those men talking to your foster-brother?' asked a man from Liscannor, a sea-port a few miles away. Others of his kin-group were with him, seven men in all, and they surrounded me.

I shrugged. 'I don't know,' I said. 'I've never seen them before, but I think they're fishermen.'

Angry faces stared at me. 'They're not fishermen,'

said another man. 'They didn't even know the names of the fish they were selling.'

'Last week the convent at Kilshanny was raided – all the silver was stolen from it,' said a third.

I gazed at him, puzzled. The convent of Kilshanny was near Liscannor, but I couldn't see what that had to do with the fishermen talking to Conan.

'They look like Thomond men to me,' said a fourth man.

'They must have come in from the sea, down the Shannon. They're here to plunder our kingdom,' said the first man.

'We'll have to set a watch on the coast; they'll never get in that way again,' said the second.

'Come on, you little brat,' said a fifth. 'Tell us what your brother is up to.'

He seized my hand and twisted it behind my back. The pain was agonising. I let out a mighty yell: 'Conan, help me!'

With the speed of a bolt of lightning, Conan crashed through the crowds to my side. There was a cracking sound, and my tormentor's right arm fell away uselessly; from the scream he gave, I guessed it was broken.

'Stand out of the way, Columba!' cried Conan. His voice was high and triumphant. There was even a hint of laughter in it. Conan loved a fight; I knew that. Still, I went to help him, though all the men's attention was on Conan.

He hit the first man an open-handed blow in the face; a quick movement of his leg, and the second was sprawling on the ground holding his head. A punch landed in the stomach of the third, and then the fourth was writhing in agony as well. The man who had twisted my arm was groaning and holding his broken arm with his left hand; but the last two were still full of fight, and they closed in on Conan. I locked my arms around one of them, but he threw me off, and I fell back – against Diarmuid from Drumevin. He held me firmly.

'Stay quiet now, like a good lad,' he said. 'Conan is a match for them.'

By now a crowd had gathered around, forming a ring around the fighting men as if it were one of those wrestling matches they sometimes hold at fairs. I wondered why nobody helped Conan; but then I realised that he had no need of anyone. Every muscle in his body was developed to its utmost by his years of work at the forge. He was more powerful than any of the men around. The other two men were big, but they didn't move as quickly nor as agilely as Conan. He seemed almost to fly between them; while one was still reeling from a punch, he was spinning to face the other. The crowd grew more and more excited. Some of the young men began to chant, 'Conan! Conan!'

Within minutes, Conan was the victor. Some more people from Liscannor came and dragged their wounded away. A goblet of strong mead made from fermented honey was handed to Conan, and then another one to me. I gulped it down. It was a drink fit for the gods, as the old men used to say. The crowd was still all around us; it seemed as if they were waiting for something.

Then a bearded, white-haired man came forward, carrying a small harp. He swept his hand across the strings, and as the first chord sounded everyone fell silent.

And then he began to chant. The strong mead was running through my brain and I couldn't understand all of his song, but the chorus line lodged itself in my mind: 'Conan, the fierce and turbulent . . .' I knew I would never forget this wonderful moment, standing shoulder to shoulder with my magnificent brother, Conan, the fierce and turbulent.

All the way home from Coad, we both sang snatches of the song as we staggered along. Conan had drunk goblet after goblet of the fiery mead, and he was quite drunk – and, even after just one goblet, so was I. Conan had his arm around my shoulders – we hadn't bought the new cloak, but I didn't care. I was in heaven. Even the memory of Sorcha was just a distant pain beneath the surface of my thoughts.

Chapter 5

'What's that?' said Conan, breaking off his song and stopping abruptly.

I stopped and listened. It was an evening of heavy, purple-black thunderclouds and there was very little light; I could see nothing except the dark bulk of the boundary bank on my left. At first I could hear nothing either.

'I don't know,' I said sleepily – and then suddenly, as if a bucket of cold water had been poured over my head, I did know.

'It's the sound of horses' hooves,' I whispered. 'The men from Liscannor are following us. They want revenge on you.'

Conan stopped and listened. I sensed that he was wondering whether to stand and fight.

'There must be at least ten of them,' I hissed urgently. 'We can't fight that many. They'll kill us.'

'The road to Drumevin is just down there,' whispered Conan. 'We'll turn off and wait till they've passed.' Softly he began to run along the grass verge to the stony road.

I followed him obediently; but then I grabbed his

sleeve. The moon had suddenly flashed out from behind the clouds, and ahead of me I saw the rounded shape of an ash tree close to the boundary bank, and beyond it the pale gold of a gorse bush. I remembered that day, so many years ago, when Sorcha and I had taken the calf up to Drumevin and watched the wolf escape into the land of Thomond.

'No,' I whispered. 'When they see we're not on the main road any more, they'll know we went that way. Let's hide. I know a place.'

As I led him behind the gorse bush, I prayed as hard as I could. It had been such a long time ago; the chances were that the hole would have been discovered and filled in. Or the wolf might still be living there – or, worse still, a huge wolf-trap might have been set in the hole. I had seen those traps, and the thought of what they might do to a man's leg or arm set me shivering. I prayed that the moon would stay out. At least we would not have to go in blind darkness into the wolf's hole.

'Here it is.' My words were just a breath in Conan's ear. The horses' hooves were coming nearer. I took a firm grip on his sleeve and pulled him into the hole.

We stood there for a moment. The thunderclouds had covered the moon again and there was no light;

but, to my intense relief, no wicked trap closed its jaws on us. We would go no further in unless the hoofbeats stopped nearby, I decided.

But they continued on down the road. I could feel Conan relax against me; but then he stiffened. Once again the moon's light flashed out, and there was a shout from one of the men: 'They're not here. Look – they must have turned off down that road there.'

'That'll be it,' said another voice. 'I'd say that road leads down to Drumshee. That's where they come from. Come on, lads; we'll soon find them. We'll see if he's still so "fierce and turbulent" by the time we've finished with him.' I heard a whip swishing through the air, and then a heavier sound – a blackthorn cudgel, or perhaps even a sword, striking the hedge.

We stayed very still while the noise of their laughter and drunken boasting grew fainter. Conan stirred uneasily beside me.

'Let's see if we can get further in,' he whispered in my ear. 'It won't take those fools long to discover that we're not on the Drumevin road. I'd like to be better hidden.'

'No . . .' I began, but he had gone ahead, and all I could do was follow.

'Look – there's light up ahead,' he said. His voice was excited, too excited for caution. 'I can feel air on my face. Columba, I think we're going through the bank. We're going to come out into the land of Thomond!'

In another few minutes we were both out of the passage and standing on Thomond land. The thunderclouds had blown away, and we could see as far as the distant mountains. Conan gazed all around. He was breathing hard, almost as if he had been running. He turned and faced me, and I could see the moonlight glittering in the blackness of his eyes. Suddenly he punched me playfully on the arm.

'You knew all about this, you rascal!' he said. 'When did you discover it?'

So, in whispers, I told him the whole story. I had never known him to listen so carefully to me before. I was bathed in happiness. From time to time, he threw his head back and laughed. When I told him – rather shamefacedly – that I had been scared to tell anyone in case I got a beating, and that I had made Sorcha promise that she would never reveal the secret either, he immediately reassured me.

'You did the right thing,' he said seriously. 'Knowledge is a dangerous thing sometimes, and this knowledge that you have is a dangerous secret. Never tell anyone about it, do you hear? It'll be a secret between us three.'

'Shouldn't it be sealed up?' I asked falteringly. I had often thought about this. 'Men from Thomond might discover it and come into Corcomroe.'

'No, let's just leave it. It's been there for years, and no one's discovered it,' said Conan lightly. 'Anyway, we should go back now. There's no sign of the men from Liscannor. And tonight is my birthday feast and my betrothal – we can't be late for that!'

We were very merry as we walked down the road towards Drumshee. The fumes of the mead had long since dissolved from my brain, but the narrow escape from danger had made us both slightly light-headed. I had never known Conan to be such good company to me. He had always treated me well – I was jealous of him, but he was never jealous of me – but, nonetheless, he had always treated me as a younger brother hardly worthy of his notice. But that night, the night of his seventeenth birthday, he treated me as an equal. He even wrestled with me and allowed me – I'm sure he allowed me – to throw him on the soft grass by the side of the road.

'You'll be stronger than me in a couple of years' time,' he said, picking himself up and dusting down his leather tunic.

It wasn't true, of course – I knew that; but I was drunk with happiness at hearing him say it. I pulled myself up as tall as I could and punched the air, delighting in the feel of muscles rippling on my arm. At the bottom of my heart was a little sore place whenever I thought of Sorcha, but I pushed her from my thoughts.

We went up the lane to Drumshee singing the bard's song, 'Conan the fierce and turbulent,' once again. When we reached the gate into the enclosure, Conan stopped and laid his hand on my shoulder.

'Someday, Columba, you and I will climb Mount Callan. We'll stand there together at first light, shoulder to shoulder, and we'll turn our faces to the sea and sing that song. Will you do that for me, my brother?' He looked down at me.

'Of course I will,' I said, and together we went into our house.

The house was all lit up and welcoming – though there was no welcome for me: my mother gave me a sour look, and my father looked away from me uneasily. I didn't care, though. I still felt as if a hot sun had shone on me; I was warm and contented in my new friendship with Conan. Together we went out to the well and washed ourselves. Conan ran a bone comb through his black curls and then, laughing, combed my pale-blond hair.

'We'll have to find a girl for you soon,' he said,

clapping me on the back. 'You're getting to be a good-looking fellow. Let's find you something clean to wear for tonight, anyway.'

We went back into the house, and Conan took out his saffron-yellow tunic from the chest by his bed and then found a white one for me.

'Here come Jarlath and Dervilla,' called my father, and we both went out to greet them. Dervilla exclaimed at my finery and kissed me, and Jarlath patted me gently on the back. I am ashamed to think of it now, but that night I cared nothing for either of them. All I cared about was pleasing Conan and winning his approval. And I cared about Sorcha.

When she arrived I couldn't take my eyes off her. I hadn't seen her for some months, and she had grown immeasurably more beautiful: her hair was more luxuriant, her eyes were bluer and her mouth redder than ever. She did not kiss me, though she smiled sweetly at me for a few seconds. But after those few seconds she had eyes for no one but Conan. She was beautifully dressed for the occasion: her tunic was made from the finest linen, bleached to a snowy white, and her cloak was woven from threads of purple and crimson wool.

He and she sat at the head of the table in our house. Their faces were illuminated by the candlelight, and they shone more brightly than any candle. Conan was especially magnificent that night. He wore the purple stain of a bruise on one cheekbone like a battle honour; it seemed to make him even more handsome. He told the story of the fight. My mother gave me a look of hate when he described how he had intervened to save me from the men of Liscannor, but soon she forgot me in the interest of the tale. My father sat breathless, a forgotten piece of meat cooling between his finger and his thumb, as he listened to Conan's account of the blows.

'Seven against one!' he said. 'That's a tale the bards will tell in years to come!'

'They already have,' I said. 'Sing him the song, Conan – go on, I'll sing it with you.'

So he sang the song, and I came in with the chorus of 'Conan, the fierce and turbulent'. Sorcha's cheeks grew pinker and her eyes burned with a blue fire. I have compared them to harebells; but since then I have seen the precious stone of lapis lazuli that comes from the far eastern lands – the stone the monks use for blue ink in their most precious works – and that was the intense, burning blue of Sorcha's eyes that night.

When I saw those eyes, all the happiness flooded

out of me and I was left with a great sense of loneliness and loss. I looked at my mother and she looked back at me with hate in her eyes. I looked at my father, but his eyes slid away from me and went back to Conan; there was love and pride in his face when he looked at Conan, but nothing when he looked at me. I put back my slice of meat. I could eat no more.

'Well,' said Jarlath when the song was finished, 'we must be on our way. I have a big job to start tomorrow – I'm covering a boat with leather. The boat-builder is bringing me the frame in the morning.'

He got to his feet, and he and Dervilla made their farewells. At the door he stopped and looked back at me. 'Are you coming with us, Columba? Or are you staying?'

It didn't take me long to make up my mind. 'No, I won't stay,' I said dully. 'I'll come home now.'

It was only when I was sitting beside Dervilla in the cart that I realised what I had said. But I knew it was true. Drumshee wasn't my home; Clogher was home to me now. My future lay with Jarlath and Dervilla.

I reached over and touched Jarlath on the shoulder. 'I've made up my mind, Jarlath,' I said quietly. 'I want to be a leather-worker, and I want to be your foster-son – if you still want me.'

'It is our greatest wish,' said Jarlath gently. 'We could ask for no better son. We both love you as if you were our own.'

Dervilla said nothing; but she kissed me and put her arm around me, just as she had on that day when I was five years old and sitting beside her with Honey on my lap.

Chapter 6

The next morning when I got up, the thought of Sorcha still lay like a heavy lump of iron in my heart; but I tried to ignore it, and I whistled cheerfully to myself as I went in to breakfast. Dervilla had put honey and a drop of cream on my porridge, and both she and Jarlath wore such an air of happiness that I swore to myself that I would be a good foster-son to them, would always do everything that was asked of me and would care for them well in their old age.

Dualta, the boat-builder, came in that morning with the boat-frame he had made from oak and ash. Jarlath's eyes widened at the size of it.

'It must be at least twelve paces long,' he said. 'What does Father Brendan want with a boat that size? I understood that there were only four of them going to Iona.'

Dualta shrugged. 'Five, he told me. I said to him, "I have to make it either for four or for six," and he said, "Let it be for six." So that's the way I made it.'

'Strange,' said Jarlath, still puzzled. 'I thought it was just going to be himself, Brother David, Brother

57

Enda and that new young fellow, Brother Ciaran. The other monks are surely too old for a journey like that.'

'From here to Iona is nothing these days,' said Dualta knowledgeably. 'The monks do it without even thinking about it. I have a cousin up in Mayo, and he says the monks there are always going to Iona. It was a monk called Columba who first set up a foundation there – did you know that?' he asked, turning to me.

I nodded silently. I knew who the extra place in the boat was for, too. Father Brendan never took no for an answer. On several occasions he had mentioned the idea of me becoming a priest and coming to Iona with him, and he had taken very little notice of my refusals. I would be useful to him on the journey. He knew that I could row; and Jarlath and I were always out fishing on Lickeen Lake, or on the ocean at Liscannor Bay. Yes, I would be useful on that journey to Iona. I swore to myself that I wouldn't go. I would stay with Jarlath and Dervilla and give back to them some of the love they had given to a lonely and unloved child.

'I'd say we'll be needing about fifty skins to cover this frame,' said Jarlath, turning back to the work in hand. 'What do you think, Columba?'

'Fifty at least,' I said briefly.

'It's lucky I had your help with all those hides,' said Jarlath, moving across to the huge vats where the hides were curing in a liquid made from oak bark and water.

A warm feeling came over me, and the hard lump in my heart seemed to melt a little. It was nice to be appreciated. It was true that I had worked hard on those ox-skins. First we had cured the skins in salt water, brought in barrels from the nearby sea; then we had washed them clean in the water of the River Fergus; then we had soaked them in lime and water, to remove the pieces of flesh that still clung to them. After that, they had gone into the tanning vats. Now they would be hung on the fence so that the water could drip from them. They couldn't be left drying for too long, or they would become stiff and difficult to sew together.

'How long will you take?' asked a voice from behind us. Jarlath and Dualta turned, but I knew who it was. I had seen him coming, but had deliberately turned my back.

'Father Brendan! You gave me a start,' said Dualta. 'What do you think of the frame?'

'She looks a fine boat,' said Father Brendan. 'How long before she's ready to sail, Jarlath?' he repeated.

I felt his eyes burning into the back of my head, though I pretended to be busy running my hand over the curved ribs of ash.

'Should be about three weeks,' said Jarlath, considering. 'What do you think, Columba? We think it'll need about fifty skins, Father. They'll all have to be sewn together, and then there'll be the sails to do as well.'

'Can't it be done any faster?' asked Father Brendan impatiently. 'I'm anxious to start; I want to be away before the autumn storms come.'

'We'll do our best,' said Jarlath with his usual grave courtesy. 'I'm lucky to have Columba. He's a very quick worker – without him, it would take months.'

'Well, then, Columba, I'll excuse you from your Latin lessons until the boat is done,' said Father Brendan graciously. 'You'll have plenty of time to make them up afterwards.'

'But . . .' said Dualta, puzzled. I knew what he was thinking: surely Father Brendan would set off as soon as the boat was covered with the skins; the day after it was ready, it could be taken to Liscannor by cart and launched on the sea. How could he go on with my Latin lessons then? I knew what the priest meant, of course – and so, I think, did Jarlath. Anyway, he gave Dualta a quick look and a slight shake of his head, and the boat-builder said no more.

I worked with great goodwill on the boat. Father Brendan was right – if he didn't go soon, he would have to wait until next summer; and I was sick of him. He was forever hanging around and telling me about the great St Columba, how wonderful the life of a priest was, and how easy and pleasant copying manuscripts would be compared to the dirt and stink of leather-working. I shut my ears to him. I was determined to stay with Jarlath and Dervilla. It didn't matter that a leather-worker only had an honour-price of one *sét*; if that was good enough for Jarlath, the noblest man I knew, it was good enough for me.

So, after two weeks of working night and day, the boat was finished. Dervilla had helped with the sail, and together we were fixing it to the mast when Conan came up the hill. 'Let me help with that,' he said, and took the mast from Dervilla. I put the last few stitches into the sails, securing them to the rigging, and the boat was finished.

'Let me give you a hand getting it on the cart,' Conan said to Jarlath.

Jarlath had planned to get several men around to help us with that, but he and I went to the prow, and Conan, with his massive back and shoulders, took the whole weight of the stern. He straightened without difficulty, walked steadily over to the cart and hoisted his end onto it; then he came around and helped Jarlath and me with the prow. We had added several planks to the cart, but the boat still overhung it on both sides.

'Let's go tell the good Father that his boat is ready, Columba,' said Conan with his ready smile, and together we walked across the hill and into the monks' enclosure.

'Come and see the boat, Father,' Conan said, putting his head into the scriptorium where Father Brendan and two other monks were working.

'Glory be to God! Is it finished?' Father Brendan jumped to his feet, almost upsetting a pot of precious gold ink. He ran out of the scriptorium and towards the abbot's house. 'Father Abbot!' he shouted. 'The boat is finished!'

The abbot came out of his house. 'Ring the bell, my son,' he said to Conan, who was smiling broadly at all the excitement. 'Ring the bell and summon the other Brothers from the fields. I must go down and bless the boat.'

'Where's the bell-rope?' Conan asked me as the abbot sped off.

'Up in the tower. We'll have to take the ladder from under the abbot's roof,' I told him. 'They keep it there so nobody will notice it. The thatch hides it.'

The ladder was slung on special hooks under the broad eaves of the thatch. You would have to be right underneath it to see it. 'Why do they go to so much trouble to hide a ladder?' asked Conan, as he carried it easily across to the belltower.

'Well, they have all their valuable treasures in the belltower,' I explained. 'The jewelled cross the king gave them, the silver book-shrine, the gold Mass-cups . . . Remember I told you about all the treasures they have?'

'I just didn't know they kept them in the belltower. I imagined they'd be in the church,' said Conan. 'Come on, climb up with me and show me.'

So Conan placed the ladder against the tower, and together we climbed up to the door, high above our heads, and into the warm, dusty, dimly lit interior of the belltower. Conan gave the bell-rope a couple of pulls; when the noise had died away, he turned to me expectantly. 'Where are they, then? I can't see anything – no chest or anything.'

'Don't tell anyone I showed you,' I warned. I went over to the side wall and began to climb the stone steps that led to the top of the belltower. It was a long climb – about a hundred steps; I was out of breath when we reached the top, but Conan was as fresh as if he had only walked down a lane.

'Up here!' he marvelled. 'Who ever would have guessed?'

I went over to the window on the east side and looked out. All of the monks were trooping down towards the boat; Father Brendan was already there, and young Brother Ciaran with him. Father Brendan was patting the boat as if it were a living creature.

I turned back to Conan. 'Put your hand on that stone there,' I said quietly. 'You see the one with the tiny cross scratched on it? Well, lift it out.'

In silence he did as I told him; and then he gasped. Beyond the stone was a large hollow space, beautifully cut into the thickness of the wall. Inside it the treasures of the monks were piled up. The jewelled cross was there; two gold Mass-cups, both studded with jewels, and a Mass-plate to match each one; the silver book-shrine; the brooch that the abbot wore on his cloak on great occasions; and, as well, a leather bag full of silver pieces. Conan looked and looked, and his eyes glittered with excitement.

'We'd better go down,' I said. 'They'll be back soon. I shouldn't have shown you, really. Father Brendan only showed me because he's sure that I'm going to join their order and become a priest.'

Conan laughed heartily – so heartily that I could

hear the sound bouncing off the circular wall all around us. 'You a priest!' he said, and punched me jovially on the arm. 'You a priest! A good-looking fellow like you! Listen, Columba, would you like to come to the fair at Coad again on Sunday? I've got a job to finish off for some men; I'm going to meet them on Sunday, and then we can go on to the fair. It won't be as good as the Lunasa one, but we'll find a nice girl for you. And, remember, I owe you a cloak. With all the excitement at Lunasa, I forgot to buy it for you.'

He was a great man to raise your spirits. As I went down the steps after him, I began to feel better. Father Brendan's offer had been at the back of my mind; but now I was certain that I would never accept it. I would stay here. I would be a help and a comfort to Jarlath and Dervilla, I would be friends with Conan, and – who knew? – I might find a girl who would love me, a girl who wouldn't mind marrying a leather-worker whose father had disowned him.

'Listen, Columba,' said Conan, as we walked back to Jarlath's house, 'don't let the priest bully you. You don't want to go to Iona. You don't want to be a monk. I'll tell you what – your job is finished here; Jarlath won't mind if you spend the day at Drumshee tomorrow. In fact, you can stay overnight if you like, and then we can go to the fair together on Sunday. You can give me a hand with some knives and throwing-spears I'm making. Father and Mother have gone to visit her sister; I'm all on my own at Drumshee. We'll be good company for each other.'

I promised. It would be just as well to be out of Father Brendan's way. The boat was finished earlier than he had expected – there was no hope of him being ready to leave the next day; and Sunday, of course, was impossible. No priest would dream of starting a journey on a Sunday. I would keep out of his way, and with any luck he would go on Monday. Jarlath would give me Saturday off very readily – he knew how I had worked day and night on that boat – and Sunday was always a holiday anyway; no one worked on Sunday. I would go to Drumshee and help Conan. I was proud that he felt I could help him at the forge; he must think I had grown quite strong.

Chapter 7

As I had thought, Jarlath made no objection to me having Saturday off. He patted me on the back and told me to go and enjoy myself, and Dervilla packed a basket of honey-cakes and little pork pies for Conan's and my dinner.

By the time I arrived Conan had the forge furnace blazing merrily, and a pile of iron lumps, smashed out of the iron-rich stones around Drumshee, was ready and waiting for us. It was my job to keep the bellows going, adding air to the fire and keeping the flames burning fiercely, and also to throw the lumps onto the fire. After about half an hour they were glowing red and starting to run; Conan raked out the iron ore and, with a heavy sledgehammer, beat the impurities – such as pieces of stone – out of the iron. Then it was put back into the fire, and then he beat it again. Only when he was satisfied that all the impurities were gone did he start to shape the knife, folding the metal – cooling, but still soft – over and over and then beating it into shape. By the time we stopped for our dinner, we had made five or six knives.

'Only four more to go,' said Conan cheerfully, as he bit into a pork pie and washed it down with some ale.

'Who wants all those knives?' I asked curiously, looking at them. They lay on the wall, shining with that blue-black sheen that iron has when it is new from the fire and the water.

'Oh, some men up Derrynahilla way,' said Conan.

Derrynahilla was a townland beyond Drumevin. I was puzzled; why would they need so many knives all at once? 'Are they preparing for a raid up that way, then?' I asked, trying to think who lived in Derrynahilla.

'That's it,' said Conan. 'I'll tell you what, Columba,' he went on, changing the subject in the careless way he had, 'I'll buy you a new tunic at the fair, as well – I owe you some silver for all the help you've given me.'

'I've done nothing,' I protested. 'I only helped with the fire.'

'Well, you're going to do something now,' said Conan, pulling me to my feet. 'You're going to make the next knife all by yourself. Come on – no excuses; you know you can do it.'

So, while Conan worked the bellows, I dropped

the iron lumps into the red–hot flames, pulled out the molten iron and wielded the heavy sledgehammer, glorying in the strength of my muscles. Then I beat the iron into the shape of a knife, and cooled it in the tub of well-water that stood beside the forge. And there it lay – my knife!

When Conan went to get some more iron ore, I quickly took my own knife from my pouch and inscribed it with a tiny dove, the symbol of St Columba that I used to draw on my little books and ink-pots when I was a child and played with Sorcha in the underground room at Drumshee. Conan noticed nothing when he came back, and I was glad: I was already a little ashamed of having marked the knife. He praised the knife, though, and even said he thought it was the best one of the lot. Then he put on his leather apron again, and I went back to working the bellows to keep the fire burning hot and bright. In less time than it had taken me to make one knife, Conan had turned out three more and four throwing-spears.

We were very merry together that night. Conan had some mead, and he shared it generously with me. In the firelight, he told me all his plans for the future.

'I'm going to be an important man, Columba,' he boasted. 'I'm going to build a big new house for myself and Sorcha. I'll have seven sons, and we'll build up this forge to be the most important one in the kingdom of Corcomroe.'

Smiling to himself, he poured another goblet of mead and offered me some. I shook my head. The old melancholy was beginning to creep over me. What sort of future would I have? I would be scratching a living as a leather-worker – Jarlath was not an old man; it would be a long time before I could do anything but live on his charity. And would any woman really want to marry me? Somehow I couldn't imagine it. Leaving Conan to his mead and his dreams by the fire, I crept across the room, threw myself on a bed and fell asleep.

★ ★ ★

The next morning, Conan and I went to Mass at Clogher. Afterwards, while Conan chatted with some other young men, Father Brendan came swiftly across the grass in front of the church and stood by my side.

'I've been looking everywhere for you, Columba,' he said gravely. 'We'll be leaving on Monday – Brother David, Brother Enda, young Brother Ciaran and I.'

70

I nodded, and hoped he would leave it at that – and that he would be gone early on Monday, so I wouldn't have to see him again. I was so used to obeying him, to feeling grateful towards him – and it was true that I owed him all of my education – that I feared I wouldn't be able to withstand him if he pressed me.

'There is room for another man in the boat,' he continued.

I nodded again. I knew that, and he knew I did. This was a six-man boat.

'Columba, I would like you to come with us,' he said, slowly and gravely. I opened my mouth, but he held up his hand for silence. 'Wait,' he said. 'I don't want you to answer now. I want you to think about it, pray about it, today. Come to me tomorrow morning and give me your answer.' Then he turned his back and went into the church.

I think he expected me to follow him, but I rushed gladly away and joined Conan. He continued talking, but threw a careless arm around my shoulders. His friends were all older than I, all boasting about girls and fights and their prowess on the hurley field and the vast amounts of drink they had consumed the night before. I tried to join in, but it was all false. I was happier talking to Dervilla and

Jarlath – happier even working in the scriptorium, copying the beautiful paintings and lettering of the sacred books and slipping in, from time to time, a minute white dove in the margin of the page.

'Come on, Columba,' said Conan after a while. 'We have some goods to deliver. See you at Coad later on, lads.'

So we made our way back to Drumshee and filled our leather satchels with the throwing-spears and knives, and set off up the hill. As we passed dwelling after dwelling in Drumevin and in Derrynahilla, I grew more and more curious. I knew that area – Drumevin better than Derrynahilla – but I couldn't think who would want all those spears and knives. It would need a big kin-group to want all that.

'Where are we going?' I asked as we passed Knockalunkard. 'There's only old Carny living up here, and he's on his own.'

'Oh, we're just meeting them on the road,' Conan said casually. I knew by his manner, though, that he didn't want me to ask any more questions, so I walked by his side in silence.

We had reached the boundary bank when I saw the men we had come to meet. They weren't from anywhere nearby; I knew everyone from our area. I said nothing, though; I just stood silently by and took the knives from my satchel when Conan asked for them.

'Walk on towards Coad, Columba,' he said cheerfully. 'I'll catch you up in a few minutes.'

I walked on; but when I had gone about a hundred paces, I couldn't resist a quick glance over my shoulder. They were talking, head close to head, and then Conan straightened up and I saw one of the men pass him a small bag. He put it in his pouch; a moment later, I heard him running down the road after me.

He was in a great mood. As we neared Coad he began to hum to himself, and I took up the tune and began to sing the words of the bard's song: 'Conan, the fierce and turbulent . . .' We met some of his friends outside the fair, and they too began to sing the song; then they lifted Conan high on their shoulders and carried him through the fair, all of us singing triumphantly. Some of the men from Liscannor were there, and they looked on in sullen silence.

They finally put Conan down by the place where the roast pork was being cooked over a great fire. 'The champion's portion!' shouted John, one of Conan's friends, and the man cooking the pig obligingly cut off a huge slab of haunch and put it, dripping fat and searingly hot, into Conan's hand.

I wondered how he could hold it – the smoke was still rising from it – but he bit into it instantly, and then took a draught of the ale that had been placed in his left hand. In three large bites the pork was finished; Conan tossed the bone to a hungry dog that hovered nearby, wiped his fingers on the grass and then threw an arm over my shoulders.

'Come on, brother,' he said, laughing. 'Let's buy you some clothes, and then we'll find you a bride.'

So, from the leather bag in his pouch, he paid for a splendid purple cloak for me, and then a tunic dyed blue with woad. 'That matches his eyes,' he said with a wink at the girl who was selling the linen tunics. I was too shy to do more than steal a glance at her, but it didn't matter anyway; she was too busy looking at Conan, in all his beauty, to spare me a glance.

Everywhere we went in the fair, people cheered and clapped Conan on the back and bought drinks for him. The news of the great fight had spread all through the kingdom. People even bought me drinks – 'You're fourteen years old, you're a man now,' said Diarmuid of Drumevin. By the time we set out on our walk home – me dressed in all my new finery, with my old clothes stuffed into my satchel – we were both quite merry, and we sang the whole way down the road.

I was cold sober by the time we reached Drumshee, though – at least, I was sober enough to shake my head when Conan asked me whether I was coming up to the house. He didn't want me to come, I could tell; and I didn't want to go either. I could see a light in my father and mother's house, and I knew they were home. They wouldn't welcome me.

'No,' I said. 'I'll go home.'

It was the second time I had called Clogher 'home', and I meant it. I really meant that Clogher would be my home for ever more, that I would throw in my lot with Jarlath and Dervilla; that I would be to them, in all matters, a son; that their cares would be my cares, their sorrows my sorrows, their injuries my injuries.

Chapter 8

It was Honey who woke me, barking a warning. He barked so seldom that I took it seriously. In a moment I was out of bed, lighting my candle and tugging on my breeches. I was pulling my old tunic over my head by the time Jarlath came out of the inner room.

'There's something amiss,' he said, seizing a heavy blackthorn cudgel from behind the door. 'I heard noises in the monks' enclosure. I'm going up there.' He took a pitch torch from the wall and thrust its end into the fire.

'I'll go with you,' I said, catching up another cudgel.

'Take Honey with you,' said Dervilla, anxious and pale, as she peered past the leather flap that served as a door to their room.

If she hadn't said that, would we have left Honey? Would one good thing have been saved from that black night? I think, myself, I would have been inclined to leave Honey. He was not a warlike dog; he was peaceful and loving, though loyal and quick to defend his own. Yes, I think I would have left Honey in the house with Dervilla.

But we took him, and the three of us went through the darkness to the monks' enclosure. Then came a stifled cry, and then a shriek; and then the sickening sounds of a human in his last agonies.

'What devil's work is this?' whispered Jarlath.

There on the grass, just outside his own house, lay the abbot. The white of his robe was stained with a fast-spreading reddish-black mark. The cry must have come from him, but he was silent now. His eyes were open and staring at the sky. I knelt down and held the palm of my hand before his mouth. There was no whisper of a breath; no slight moisture dampened my hand. He was dead.

On the ground around him were scattered a few loose straws. I stared at them, puzzled, and then looked up. The hooks under the thatch were bare. The ladder was gone.

And then Honey barked. It was only afterwards that I realised it was a bark of welcome. At the time I was distracted, kneeling beside the dead figure of the abbot. Honey shot away from us, still barking. Jarlath stood up. He moved forward and then hesitated, his stick swinging loosely in his right hand, the flaring torch still held high above his head.

At that moment the moon came out from behind the clouds, shedding its light on the whole scene. The ladder from the abbot's house had been moved to the round tower, under the high door. A figure was coming out of the door – a man in a short, loose cloak, the hood drawn well over his head. He climbed down the ladder backwards; he moved awkwardly, because his right hand was clutching something to his breast.

In a moment Honey had bounded up to the ladder and stood there on his hind legs, his supple, otter-like tail wagging furiously and those barks of joy shooting out from him. His weight on the ladder threw the man off his already precarious balance; he fell heavily to the ground, the precious cups and plates, the book-shrine and the brooch spilling from his hands. Honey leaped on him.

There was a flash of steel. I saw it in the moonlight, but I couldn't move. Even if I had, I would have been too late to save Honey, but perhaps I might have done some good; perhaps I might have prevented what followed. But I didn't move. I stayed still while the blood of Honey's loving heart spilled out on the grass and his great groan of agony pierced through me.

Jarlath gave a cry of anger and rushed forward. He

never hesitated. Jarlath loved Honey; he loved him with all the love that a childless man can give to a dog who takes a child's place in a household. He swung his stick. I suspect that he would have been able to kill the man who had slaughtered his dog – after all, the man was at his feet, still sprawled awkwardly on the grass. But, at the last moment, the gentleness of Jarlath's nature awoke. He struck to hurt, he struck to punish, but he did not strike to kill.

It was a mistake. When you are dealing with a killer, you do not show him mercy. In a moment the man was on his feet. Jarlath's blows seemed to have no effect on him. Once again the knife flashed; and by the time I got there, Jarlath was lying dead, with the handle of the knife sticking out of his chest.

The murderer made no attempt to remove it. Still clutching a leather bag to his chest, he began to run. From around the houses and out of the church and the belltower came other dark figures, all of them running, but I took no notice of them. I fixed my eyes on the hooded man who had just murdered Jarlath. I would allow nothing to deflect me. I was going to kill him.

He was fast, but I ran as I had never run before. The moon was almost hidden again, but there was enough light for me to see the fleeing form. From time to time he glanced over his shoulder, and I saw the flash of a throwing-spear in his hand, but he made no attempt to throw it.

The other men were gaining on me; they would catch me if I did not do the deed quickly. I pulled a last few measures of strength from my tired legs. I bounded forwards, raised the heavy blackthorn cudgel and brought it down on the back of the man's head.

He did not fall. I couldn't imagine how anyone could stand up to the force of that blow – it had all my strength behind it – but he only turned, the throwing-spear in his hand. Then his arm dropped to his side. I didn't give him a second chance. Once again I raised the cudgel and brought it down on his head. This time he dropped like a stone, and I knew he was dead. No one could live with a skull crushed like that.

The other men, his companions, were close behind me. I waited. Jarlath was dead and Honey was dead: I didn't care if these raiders killed me or took me prisoner. At least I had taken revenge on the murderer of those I had loved.

To my surprise, the men simply passed me by. Clearly they put no value on this hooded man; he must have been an outsider, not one of their kin-group. I knelt beside him as the noise of their running feet died away. They were going in the direction of Thomond, I thought, as I pushed back the hood from the man's face.

And then the moon came back out from the clouds. It shed its merciless, cold white light over the scene. Lying on the grass at my knees was no stranger, no man from Thomond. It was Conan. Thick, black-looking blood was clotting his black curls; his brown eyes were beginning to glaze over, and the colour was dissolving and seeping out of his face. It was Conan; and I, his foster brother – I who had loved him so much – I had killed him.

Chapter 9

Over the next few days, whenever I thought about that terrible night, one thing was clear in my mind. Conan had known that it was me; he had known, and that was why he hadn't used his throwing-spear. He hadn't wanted to kill his brother. But I, his brother, had killed him.

No one knew what I had done. Not at the beginning, anyway.

I left him lying there and went back to the monks' enclosure. I gathered up Jarlath's body in my arms. The monks had come out by then, but none of them stopped me. I took him across the fields to the little house where Dervilla stood in the doorway, her hands pressed against her mouth. I placed him gently on the bed. I could not bear to watch his wife's grief, so I went across to the monks' enclosure and carried Honey back to the house where he had been loved so much. His fur was still warm; I buried my face in it, and for the first time that night I wept. I wept for him, for Jarlath, for myself, and I wept for the gentle abbot. But I did not weep for Conan. I couldn't. My heart was hardened against him. All I could think of was what he had done to me by killing two creatures whom I had loved, who had loved me.

His body was taken to the house at Drumshee, and candles were burned around it. Sorcha came and mourned, her eyes swollen and her beauty hidden. No one knew what Conan had been doing in the monks' enclosure that night.

'He must have heard something when he was coming home late,' said my father, his voice rough and husky with tears.

'He was as brave as a lion. He would never have thought of himself. He would have gone to help the monks,' sobbed my mother. She would not eat nor sleep; she mourned day and night beside the body of her best-beloved son.

No one knew what he had done, and no one knew what I had done. All the raiders had escaped. Father Brendan praised my bravery in trying to follow the raiders. He thought I had been helping Conan. He, and all of them, thought Conan had been killed by the raiders.

'He had no knife on him,' mourned my father. 'Why didn't he have a knife? That would have been more use than a throwing-spear.'

But I knew why he had had no knife. He had left

it in Jarlath's chest. I knew what knife he had had, also. When Dervilla and I took it from Jarlath's chest I had seen the picture of the dove, the tiny symbol of St Columba, engraved on it. Jarlath and Honey had both been killed by the knife I had forged at Drumshee. I was, indeed, the devil's child.

I stayed away from Drumshee; I could not bear it. I dug a grave for Honey just outside the monks' enclosure and laid him in the black, peaty earth. Then I dug a grave for Jarlath inside the enclosure. My father and his brother Aidan came to dig the grave for Conan. He and Jarlath would both be buried the next day, on Tuesday. There would be one more night of prayers, one more night of tears, and then the burial. The two men – one gentle and honourable, the other a thief, a liar and a murderer – would lie side by side, and no one else would ever know the truth of how they had died.

It was about an hour past midnight on that last night when Dervilla broke through my wall of silence.

'What's the matter, Columba?' she said, and the tenderness of her voice made tears start to my eyes again. 'There's something very badly wrong. It's not just sorrow? You've been like a son to me all these years; I know when something is wrong.'

I shook my head. I couldn't lie, but I couldn't tell her.

She was silent for a while; then she laid her hand gently on the cold, white face of what had been Jarlath, her loving husband. 'If he were alive,' she said gently, 'he would advise you. There is something worrying you. You look frightened.'

'I can't say,' I blurted out. 'I can't tell anyone. It's a sin that I can't talk about.'

I wondered whether she would guess that I was guilty of the worst sin of all. I was guilty of the murder of my foster-brother. Under the law, that crime meant that I should be banished from the kingdom – perhaps even put into a boat with no oars and launched out to sea to die of thirst or drowning.

'Why don't you tell the priest?' said Dervilla. 'He'll keep your secret, but he will absolve you from your guilt.'

Suddenly I felt better. I knew that was the right thing to do. My mind was in such turmoil that I couldn't tell how guilty I was. Part of me was saying: *I didn't mean to do it, it was an accident; and he had just killed my foster-father* . . . But the other half of my mind kept repeating over and over again, without any pity: *You're a murderer; you murdered your own foster-brother. And it was you who brought the raiders to the monks' enclosure. If you had never shown him the secret way to Thomond, he would never have been tempted, would never have brought death to Jarlath and Honey.*

Father Brendan would know what was right. He was still there; because of the abbot's death, he and the other monks had postponed their journey until Wednesday. I would talk to him. He might tell me that it had been no sin; at worst, he would give me a penance, and then I would be absolved.

'I'll see him at dawn,' I said. Then I fell on my knees and prayed for Jarlath's gentle soul, that he might be happy in heaven, and for Dervilla, that she would find comfort in time; and I prayed for Honey, my golden dog.

When dawn came I got up from my knees and walked stiffly across to the monks' enclosure. The monks were just going into their little church for the morning prayers. I knelt at the back of the church and joined in with the Latin responses. My mind had grown clearer. The sorrow was still there, but the terrible guilt had eased a little.

When the service was over, I went to Father Brendan and caught him by the sleeve. 'Father, I need to speak to you,' I said.

This was where I made my mistake. If I had asked him to hear my confession, he would have been bound to secrecy by all the vows he had taken when he became a priest. If I had asked him to hear my confession, none of what followed would have happened. I would have stayed there, comforted Dervilla, looked after her, worked at the leather-making – perhaps even, in time, become a son to my father and my mother.

But I didn't say the word 'confession'. When Father Brendan said, 'Yes, my son?' and sat down on a bench, I just knelt beside him and told him the whole story. I kept nothing back. I told him how I had shown the monks' treasure to Conan; I told him about the way through the boundary bank to Thomond, about how Conan had been talking with the strange men at the fair, about the knives we had made together – knives that Conan had sold to the men of Thomond.

'And, Father,' I said, my voice breaking in a sob, 'when I helped Dervilla to wash Jarlath's body, the dagger we took from his heart was the dagger I made – it had my mark on it, the dove of St Columba. I am responsible for Jarlath's death.'

Then I broke down and sobbed. He let me cry for a few minutes; then he said gently, 'What happened to Conan?'

I knew that I had come to the end; soon the worst

thing of all would be told. My voice did not falter. 'I killed him with my stick, Father. I killed my own foster-brother.' I bowed my head and waited.

He laid his hand on my head for a moment. Then he spoke. 'You know what Christians say, Columba? A life for a life.'

I nodded. I didn't care. I would have been glad if he had taken out a dagger and killed me as I knelt there at his feet. No pain could be worse than the pain I had been suffering for the last few days.

'You took Conan's life,' he went on. 'Now you must give God yours in exchange. This is the price you must pay: you must come with me to Iona tomorrow. The monks call it the "green martyrdom", exile from your own land. Will you promise?'

'I promise,' I said in a dull voice. What else could I say? He was right – it was God's law: a life for a life.

I got up and went home. 'Are you happier now?' Dervilla asked when I came in. I nodded. I didn't know whether I was happier or not. I didn't feel as if I could ever be happy again. I was more at peace with myself, at least; I suppose that was something.

'Yes,' I said dully. 'I'm going to go to Iona with Father Brendan.'

'Oh,' she said, one soft sound and then no more.

'What will you do?' I asked, suddenly realising

what this would mean to her.

'I think I'll go and live with my brother for a while. He's a leather-worker, too; maybe one of his sons will come here when he's a bit older.'

I had no more feeling left in my heart. I just nodded again.

'Father Brendan said to tell you he'll send three of the younger monks to help me carry Jarlath's body over to the enclosure,' I said. 'We must prepare a litter for him to lie on.'

So the next few hours were filled with this. I took two long, straight ash saplings, each the length of a man, and stitched thongs of leather between them to join them into a litter. I had some foolish thought that he would lie more happily on the material that he had worked with all his life. He had never thought much of wood or iron; leather was everything to him. Dervilla covered his body with linen wrappings, and then brought flowers from the meadow and made the litter a thing of beauty. It was, I suppose, the last tribute that her love could pay to him.

I worked with her. I worked willingly – almost happily, oddly enough. Something had come into my head, some little thread of hope. Perhaps my father wouldn't allow Father Brendan to take me to Iona. After all, I was still a child. I belonged to my father until I was seventeen; that was the law. If I spoke to my father after the burial, he might tell Father Brendan that I couldn't go, that I didn't want to be a priest – even, perhaps, that he and my mother didn't want me to go. Perhaps even – but here my imagination failed me – that they wanted me to come back to Drumshee and fill the empty place.

Chapter 10

Just before noon the three young monks arrived, and together the four of us carried Jarlath's body across the field, to the little burial place within the monks' enclosure. Dervilla followed behind. She did not weep, but there was such sadness, such emptiness in her face that I could not bear to look at her. We stood beside the grave, a light mist blowing from the west and dampening our faces.

Father Brendan began the ceremony. For a moment I caught a startled look on Dervilla's face: we had both assumed that Conan and Jarlath would be buried at the same time, that it would be a joint ceremony; but Father Brendan, without waiting for my family to arrive with Conan's body, launched straight into the great solemn prayer beseeching God's compassion in transporting this soul to heaven above. He seemed to have assumed direction and control of the monks since the abbot's death. The monks raised their voices in that sorrowful hymn 'De Profundis', and slowly and gently Jarlath was lowered into the ground.

Dervilla leaned over and cast the first handful of earth on the body. She turned away while I covered him, as carefully and reverentially as I could. I felt her pain like a wound in my own body, but there was nothing I could do, no comfort I could give her. I let her go back to the house by herself. I couldn't go with her: I had to stay and see Conan buried.

At last we heard the voices. They were coming along the flat ground of Ballagh. Even at that distance, I heard my mother's voice raised in the keen of a woman mourning her dead child. I finished my task at the graveside before turning around. I was glad that Father Brendan had chosen to have separate ceremonies. Jarlath had been buried with quiet dignity; Conan's burial would be a noisy outpouring of raw grief.

Father Brendan waited. Even now I feel a sense of astonishment when I think of how he waited there that day, tall, impassive, his long white robe fluttering in the hilltop breeze. He waited while the crowd – my parents, Conan's own parents, Sorcha and her parents, all the young men of the neighbourhood – came wailing up the hill, pushing the small handcart with Conan's body upon it. He waited until the handcart with its tragic burden came close to him. Then he glanced down. Conan's body was heavily swathed in linen, but his face was uncovered and he looked as I had often seen him look – as if he had just fallen asleep.

'This man cannot be buried here in this holy ground,' said Father Brendan. He said it quietly and simply, with no great emphasis, but all the wailing and keening stopped like the noise of a storm wind stops when you shut the house door upon it.

'This man was a murderer, a thief and a liar,' continued Father Brendan, still in that grave, low voice. 'He lied to his family and to his priests. He stole the property of God from His holy churches – and, only a few nights ago, he killed our Father Abbot. I say to you: take this body hence! Brand him as a murderer and an outcast! Take him to the outer bounds of the kingdom of Corcomroe – the kingdom he sought to despoil. Let his corpse rot there, as an example to all men of the evil that can come about when a man covets gold that is not his!'

No one spoke. They hardly breathed. The men pushing the handcart let go of the handles; one by one, they all turned and went back down the hill. The three sets of parents were left there – my parents, Conan's, Sorcha's; and Sorcha herself, a frozen statue of grief.

'Is this true?' asked Conan's father, Fiachra,

eventually. He was Conan's blood father, but I don't think his love for Conan was as great as the love that my own parents had borne him.

I said nothing. My mother's face was grey. My father looked like a man who had been struck a great blow. Conan's mother was weeping.

'It is true,' said Father Brendan gravely.

'But, Father,' persisted Fiachra, 'who told you this story? How do you know it's true?'

I looked at my father, and suddenly I knew that he believed the story. He had known all the time what Conan was doing. It was impossible that Conan should have been supplying the Thomond men with weapons, should have had so much silver to spend, without my father, at least, guessing his secret. He must have watched him work at the forge, turning out those knives and throwing-spears. I saw all this in his bent head and his averted eyes.

Perhaps, I thought suddenly, *perhaps now everything will be different*. Perhaps he would turn away from his love for his foster-son; perhaps he would feel such disgust for what Conan had done that he would turn back to his own flesh-and-blood son. Father Brendan had only to say, 'I know it is true,' and my father would believe him.

But Father Brendan did not say those words. I

know, now, why he didn't – why he said what he did say. I know now that he was determined to get me to come to Iona with him; and so he spoke the words that were to banish me from Drumshee.

'Columba told me,' he said. 'Columba saw him sell the weapons to the men from Thomond. Columba saw him kill our Father Abbot, and then he saw him kill that good man, Jarlath.' He paused; then he added, 'Columba killed Conan, but that was not murder. That was Conan's punishment. That was revenge. I have given Columba a penance for that killing, but I don't regard it as murder.'

My mother screamed. I don't think I'll ever forget that scream. It rang from hill to hill; no banshee ever uttered a more fearsome shriek. 'You devil's brat!' she spat. Then she fell on me, kicking and spitting and clawing at my face and eyes.

'Take her away,' said Father Brendan authoritatively to my father, and he seized my mother by the arms and began to drag her down the hill. When he had gone a few steps, he turned and spoke to me.

'Never come back to Drumshee,' he said. 'Never come back to Drumshee. There's no place for you there. Drumshee will never be yours.'

Then he turned back to my mother, and together

they went slowly down the hill. I caught a look of satisfaction on Father Brendan's face. Now he was sure of me.

'Go now, all of you,' said Father Brendan, looking at Conan's parents and Sorcha and her parents. 'Columba will take Conan's body and lay it on the boundary bank. That will be part of his penance.'

Conan's parents left immediately. I watched them go down the hill, their heads hanging with the heavy shame of what their son had done. Sorcha still stood frozen; she had neither moved nor cried out. Her face was bleached white and her eyes seemed to have lost their colour.

'Come on,' said her father roughly. Her mother put an arm around Sorcha, but her father was angry. This would do his daughter no good. She had lost one husband-to-be, and she would be lucky to find another: the people around would shy away from all the families now. Conan's deeds were a disgrace to all of us.

I waited until they had gone before I began to move. I waited, too, for Father Brendan to go.

'I will see you tomorrow morning on Liscannor beach,' he said eventually. I nodded. I didn't care. I might as well go to Iona as anywhere else.

He looked closely at me and then walked off

towards the church. When he had disappeared, I went up to the shed behind the house and found Jarlath's spade. I took it back to the graveyard and laid it on the handcart beside Conan's body. One thing I was determined upon: whatever Father Brendan ordered, whatever the Church might decree, I would bury Conan's body. I would not leave him to rot, exposed to the gaze of all men; to be torn apart by foxes and wolves, his eyes pecked out by the great grey crows. If I could not give him a Christian burial, at least I could lay him in the earth.

I was trudging down the road towards Ballinacurra crossroads, pushing the handcart before me, when I heard shouting from the road that leads to Moughna and Mount Callan. I stopped to listen. The words came clearly through the quiet air. It was Sorcha's father.

'If you go back to Drumshee now, you can stay there!' he shouted. 'I'll have nothing more to do with you. It will be hard enough to get you married as it is; if you go back there, you'll be stained forever with their disgrace.'

I stopped and strained my ears. Sorcha was saying something, but her words were drowned by the noisy sobs of her mother. What would she decide? It was nothing to me – I was banished – but somehow I liked to think of her at Drumshee.

'Go, then, for the evening,' came her father's angry voice. 'And remember: if you're not back home tomorrow morning, never come in my door again.'

I waited. She came down the road towards me, walking slowly with her head bent, and as she drew near I saw the silent tears flowing down her cheeks. I stiffened. Would she, too, curse and swear at me; disown me forever as my own parents had? What would she say to me, who had killed the love of her life?

'Kill me,' she said, her voice harsh and rough with pain. 'You killed him; kill me now. Look, your knife is at your waist. Do it now and put me out of my misery.'

I put my hand on her arm. She looked at it dully, almost as if she expected to see a knife in it.

'Sorcha,' I said, 'I want to bury Conan. I don't want to leave his body out on the boundary bank for the wild animals and the crows. I'm going to bury him at Drumshee.'

She looked at me. Her eyes were grey, all colour washed from them by sorrow. 'No,' she said. 'We'll bury him on the top of Mount Callan. He'll rest easy there, and I'll visit his grave every day.'

So all that afternoon we walked together on the

dreary road through the bog pasture. The walk, pushing that heavy handcart, took about four hours, and during all that time Sorcha said not a single word to me. She walked beside the cart, and from time to time she touched Conan's dead body, as if she could not believe that someone who had been so alive was now dead.

During that afternoon, I think, I grew from a boy to a man. I had always loved Sorcha, but it had been a boy's love — the love of a boy for his sister, for his beloved dog, for his foster-mother, for someone who was pretty and kind and warm and loving herself; all these things had been in my love. But that afternoon I glimpsed another kind of love — a passionate love that knows no bounds, is not destroyed by any failure or crime on the part of the beloved. That was the love Sorcha had had for Conan.

When we reached the bottom of Mount Callan the sun had not yet set, but it was low in the western sky. The year was beginning to turn; soon the dark days of autumn would be upon us. I looked at the sky and then at Sorcha. There would be barely time for what we had to do.

She seemed to read my thoughts; she shook her head and spoke for the first time. 'No, we'll bury him at dawn. I'll come back at dawn and we'll . . .we'll take him up to the top of the mountain.'

Her voice choked on a sob and she turned away, but after a few steps she turned back. 'There's a shepherd's hut there, just on the other side of that field. You can spend the night there. I'll call you at dawn,' she said. The words were kind, but there was no kindness in her face – just a bitter, black hatred.

★ ★ ★

And so we buried him at dawn. Over and over again, during the sleepless few hours I spent in the shepherd's hut – Conan's body lying quietly beside me, just as he had lain all those years ago when we were children together at Drumshee – I remembered what he had said about Mount Callan.

It's the best place in the world . . . Sorcha and I went up there last Sunday. We climbed right to the top, and we stood there and looked down at the ocean. The wind was in our faces, and the waves were white with foam – it looked as if a herd of wild white horses were tossing their manes down there. It's my place! I felt as if I never wanted to come down to the flat land again.

Well, he never would come down again. He would stay there until the end of the world. And it was my doing. Conan the handsome, Conan the strong, Conan the beloved, Conan the fierce and turbulent. I remembered how we had sung that song, coming down the road.

Someday, Columba, you and I will climb Mount Callan. We'll stand there together at first light, shoulder to shoulder, and we'll turn our faces to the sea and sing that song. Will you do that for me, my brother?

'I won't sing the song, Conan,' I said aloud to the silent body, 'but I'll carve those words onto a stone; and in the centuries to come, whenever men climb that mountain, they'll see those words and remember you.'

A bitter sort of peace came over me, and I shut my eyes to blot out his face. I think I dozed for a while. I didn't dream; I was afraid that I would, but I didn't. I slept very lightly, and the sound of Sorcha coming through the rushes roused me. I was at the door as soon as she was, and one glance showed me that she hadn't slept. Her beauty was dimmed, almost extinguished, but I loved her more than I ever had.

So together we climbed that mountain. Together we buried Conan.

All the way down I kept looking at Sorcha. I think I was hoping for some sign, some softening, but there was none. If she had made some move towards me then, I would never have gone. I would have stayed and hoped and worked – slaved – for her; but her heart was still full of love for Conan, and she had nothing left for me.

At the beach, we parted without a word and I gave myself up to Father Brendan.

Chapter 11

Blue sky, blue sea, a light wind blowing from the south: who could ever have guessed that a journey that started so well could end so terribly?

My mood, however, was black. In a way, it was a pity that the weather was so good. There was nothing for any of us to do once we had rowed out beyond the shoreline. The south wind filled our sails and blew us briskly up the west coast, driving us towards Iona. The three younger monks chattered excitedly, Brother Ciaran laughing like a child on a holiday, Brother David pointing out every house on the coast, Brother Enda peering over the side of the boat. Father Brendan read his prayer book and I sat in the prow of the boat, wrestling with the voice of my conscience and looking with unseeing eyes across the white-capped waves.

You have killed your brother, said the pitiless voice in my mind; and then I would hear the crack of the blackthorn cudgel, the splitting of Conan's skull. *You betrayed your friends*, continued the voice, and I would hear the terrible sound that my beautiful dog Honey had made when the knife slid under his ribs and opened up his loving heart, and I would see Jarlath the kind, Jarlath the gentle, lying there with my knife sticking out of his chest.

'There's Inishbofin, Columba,' said Father Brendan, tapping me on the arm to bring my attention back to him. 'That's the island where the monks from Iona came to make their settlement about a hundred years ago. There's Mayo, beyond it, where the English monks settled.'

I nodded absently. He had told me that story, but I couldn't be bothered trying to recall it.

'Did the blessed St Columba ever come back to Ireland himself, Father Brendan?' asked Brother Ciaran.

'Never,' said Father Brendan. 'He had sworn that his eyes would never see Ireland again. When he reached Iona, he and his twelve companions buried their boat under the sand in the bay where they landed. To this day that sacred place is called the Bay of the Coracle.'

'Are we making good time, Father?' asked Brother David hurriedly. I could see that they didn't like the story of the boat being buried. None of them wanted Father Brendan to think of doing that. Already they were beginning to miss their home place.

'We're making excellent time; God Himself has

blessed our journey,' said Father Brendan, with the usual note of self-satisfaction in his voice.

I didn't listen any more. I was back wrestling with my thoughts. *If only a storm would come up*, I thought. *If only I could be drowned in that bright-blue water, all decisions would be taken from me.*

'We're leaving Ireland now,' said Father Brendan's voice. 'There's Derry over there – that's where the blessed St Columba came from originally.'

After that there was silence. All the young monks were looking quite apprehensive now that they were leaving their home country. It was getting late – soon it would be dark, and some of us would sleep while others kept watch. Night or day, good weather or bad, it made little difference to Father Brendan. He was a man with a vision, a man driven by a dream. His life was lived for the copying of the great gospel books. Over in Iona, the work that some said had been started by the blessed St Columba himself – the most wonderful gospel book in the whole of Christendom – was nearing its close; and Father Brendan wanted a hand in it before the book was finished.

The next morning the wind continued to blow, sweeping us away from Ireland. When I looked back, I could no longer see land; but ahead of us there was a blue shape on the horizon.

'If you look carefully, you can see the land of Scotland,' said Father Brendan. '"Scots" was the old word for the Irish people, and Scotland was the land the Irish had ruled over; the kings of Scotland were part of the great O'Neill tribe, St Columba's own tribe. They speak Gaelic there, just as we do.'

'We'll soon be there,' said Brother Ciaran excitedly. 'This south wind will get us there before nightfall.'

As he said it, the weather changed. The wind dropped. The air became very still. Grey clouds began to drift across the sky.

'We'll have to row if this goes on,' I said, but I said it indifferently. I didn't care when we got to Iona; I didn't care if we never got there.

'Let's leave the sails up; there's still a bit of a breeze,' said Brother Enda. I saw him look down at his hands. Even the little rowing we had done had already blistered the soft skin of hands more used to holding a quill than an oar or a spade. These were not the monks who toiled in the fields and milked the cattle; they were educated monks. Father Brendan had brought them to work on the great gospel book of St Columba.

The hours passed. From time to time we rowed,

but we left the sails up to catch the slightest whisper of wind. Then, towards nightfall, there came a new coldness in the air. The sky darkened. The storm that I had longed for came at last.

The wind veered around, from an uncertain south breeze to a fierce, unpredictable northern gale. It whirled around us, sending the little coracle spinning like a top. The sails were worse than useless; the little boat began to tilt, and a minute later it was lying flat on its side, its heavy sails soaked in salt water. The five of us clung to the part that was still above the waves.

'Take down the sails!' screamed Father Brendan – easy for him to order, but almost impossible for us to achieve.

I slid my knife from my pouch. In a storm like this, our only chance of survival was to cut the sails loose and rely on the oars for the rest of our journey. I was clinging to the side of the boat; cautiously I let go and edged my way towards the centre. The spars that held the sails aloft were almost submerged, but they were slender hazel spars and my knife was sharp. In a minute I sliced partway through one spar. The wood cracked, then broke under the strain of its own weight; one sail floated loose and disappeared under a towering wave. I cut the second spar, then the third, and then the boat was just a shell of hazel branches covered with ox-hides.

'Move to the centre!' I cried. 'Take up your oars!'

I took two of the oars myself. I felt as though all Conan's strength, the strength that had ebbed out of his body when I killed him, had descended to me. Father Brendan and the three young monks had an oar each and the boat became a six-man boat, six oars beating against the might of the wind.

The land ahead drew closer, and Father Brendan, who had made the journey several times before, came to a quick decision. 'Row to shelter!' he yelled, above the thunder of the waves and the scream of the wind. 'Row towards the land. That's the island of Mull.'

So we rowed with all our might. I had forgotten about my momentary wish to drown: there was no thought in my mind but the struggle for life, my life and the lives of my companions.

'There's a light flashing,' shouted Father Brendan. 'Row towards the light! That's some merciful soul with a lantern showing us where to land.'

I risked a glance over my shoulder. I saw the lantern; then there was a flash of lightning, and I could see the man holding it. He was standing at the top of a cliff; there was a woman beside him, and a child – a small child. The man was pointing, pointing to a small inlet below the cliff. I snatched a second glance: yes, the inlet might offer safety for us. On either side of that curve in the towering cliffs were rocks – the sea splintered into a thousand pieces off their jagged surfaces – but, within the shelter of that little bay, the waves curved and ebbed and flowed, and nothing broke their smooth surface until they reached the cliff itself. It was possible that there was sand beneath the water, and we could beach our boat safely there.

'Row for the bay,' I yelled, and bent my back to the task.

A minute later I risked another glance behind. I could see the man more plainly, swinging the lantern with one hand and with the other pointing to the bay below. The woman was pointing as well, and so was the child, her over-large cloak fluttering in the stiff breeze.

And then, suddenly, the wind rose to a crescendo. It buffeted my face and body with such force that I was pushed forward on my oars. And we were down low, we were in the shelter of the huge cliffs; the man and his family were up at the top, unsheltered. The wind caught the child – her cloak acting like a sail – and hurled her from the cliff-top down into the sea. She fell like a bird, intent on fish, that drops from the cliff and hits the water a second later.

In that second I was out of the boat and swimming strongly towards her. It was Jarlath who had encouraged me to learn to swim; every time we had collected barrels of salt water from Liscannor, I had learned how to battle against the stormy seas of the west. But never had I battled against such a sea as this. The waves were as high as mountains, and the current was strong; it was sweeping me, and the child ahead of me, towards the rocks. She was still afloat, though. I could see her little cloak, gaily striped in reds and purples, spread out on the waves.

At that moment I thought of Conan. I thought of him without hate or bitterness, even without guilt; I thought about his strength, and even − strange that this should pass through my mind at such a time − about his kindness to me. Once again I felt the vigour of his young body flood into mine. I felt myself rise in the water with a tremendous leap, as a dolphin leaps for sport − and then I had reached the child. She was screaming, but the roar of the wind was so great that it was only when I held her little body in my arm that the silent scream became a shrill outpouring of fear.

'You're safe now,' I shouted in her ear, and prayed that it might be true.

I turned to look for the boat, but it was nowhere

near. It was being swept helplessly along; without my skill at the oars, they had little chance of controlling it. I trod the water for a moment, holding the child tightly with my left arm. It was useless to expect the boat to pick us up. It was whirling helplessly – but not towards the rocks: the current and the waves were driving it into the little bay. If the floor was sandy, all would be well. Thankfully I allowed the current to sweep me and my small burden in the same direction, kicking my legs vigorously and guiding myself with my right hand.

The boat was nearly there. The water must be quite shallow, and I wondered why they didn't swim for safety – though I knew little of any of them; perhaps they couldn't swim. At that moment, a wave almost as high as the cliff itself stole up from behind and swept me on its broad back towards the towering face of the cliff. I remember that, even in this terrible moment, I prayed for the life of the child. *Save her, Lord, and let me drown* . . . I remember this prayer in my mind; and after that I remember no more.

★ ★ ★

When I woke up the silence seemed intense, like the silence when a bell that has been jangling in your

111

ears suddenly ceases. I realised that the terrible howling of the wind and the thunder of the waves had been shut off. For a moment my eyes could pick out nothing from the warm darkness that surrounded me; but then they grew used to the dim light, and I saw that I was in a small, warm room lit by two candles made from rushes and by a wood fire that burned blue and orange in the hearth.

Father Brendan was in a chair beside the fire, his face buried in his hands. On the opposite side of the fireplace sat the woman; and in her arms, warmly wrapped in a blanket, was the child. I sat up hastily.

'The child – is she alive?' I whispered urgently.

The woman came across and sat down on the bed beside me, still holding the child. Her husband moved out of the shadows of the doorway, lit a candle from the fire and stood behind them.

'Yes, she is well,' said the woman. Smiling, she held up the child, turning the little face towards me. In the light of the candle I saw that she had corn-coloured hair, braided into two plaits, and her eyes were the blue of a summer sky. I smiled at her, reached out and touched her hand; it was warm and soft. Then she smiled back at me. She must have been about seven years old, and she had begun to shed her baby teeth; when she smiled she showed all the gaps. Suddenly I was back to that day at Drumshee, when I was six years old and Jarlath and Dervilla of Clogher came to buy a puppy. This little girl from Mull was Sorcha all over again. She had her hair, her eyes, her gap-toothed smile.

'You saved her life,' said the woman softly.

'What's your name?' I asked the child.

'Bethoc,' she whispered shyly. Then, growing bolder, she leaned from her mother's arms and pointed. 'What's that on your shoulder?'

I glanced down. The fisherman had removed my tunic; my bare shoulder showed from under the blanket, and the birthmark flickered in the light from the fire.

'I don't know,' I said. 'I was born with it when I was a little baby.'

She smiled her gap-toothed smile again. 'It's the cross of Jesus,' she said confidently. 'Are you Jesus?'

'He was sent by Jesus to save your life,' said the woman, stroking the little face beside her own.

'Lie still now – don't talk,' said her husband. 'You've had a bad blow to your head.' He touched my brow, and I felt the sharp ache. I must have hit my head against one of the rocks. Someone had roughly bandaged it with linen.

'You must lie still,' he repeated, as I struggled to sit

up. Gently he put his hand on my shoulder and pushed me back to the bed, then covered me with the rough woollen blanket.

'Sleep now,' said the woman softly, and she carried the little girl back over to the fire.

I lay there in the warm darkness, but I did not sleep. *You saved her life* . . . I knew it was true: the child would have died if I had not reached her so quickly. Bethoc: that meant 'young life'. Perhaps this would be my payment to God for the killing of Conan. *A life for a life*, Father Brendan had said. Perhaps now I had bought my freedom. I could go back to Drumshee.

I would go back to my father and mother, and I would take Conan's place at the forge. Perhaps I wasn't the devil's child after all. *Sent by Jesus*, the woman had said . . . A warm feeling came over me, and I smiled at the memory of the little girl's words. Perhaps someday my mother would give me some of the love she had given to Conan. Now, with the mind of a man, I could understand how her love for my dead brother had turned itself so strongly towards Conan that there had been none left for me; but I would win her over. And Sorcha . . . I would give her time to grieve for Conan, but I would be there for her when she was ready – and suddenly I felt confident that, after a year or two, she would turn naturally towards me. We would have children, pretty little children with blue eyes and corn-coloured hair; Drumshee would be filled with the sounds of their laughter, and none of them would ever be allowed to feel unloved even for a moment.

So I lay in that warm, woodsmoke-scented darkness and dreamed my happy dreams. And all the time the black figure of Father Brendan sat by the fire, never lifting his head from his hands.

 # Chapter 12

The next morning I found out why Father Brendan had sat there, saying nothing. The three young monks – Brother David, Brother Enda and Brother Ciaran – had all been drowned when the boat was dashed against the rocks. Father Brendan blamed himself, I suppose, looking back on it now; but then, that morning, I only felt that he blamed me. I was the strongest rower – the others had all been young scholars, good with the quill, but with no strength in their arms. If I had not jumped from the boat to rescue the child, we might have landed safely. I read condemnation in Father Brendan's cold grey eyes: *What is the life of this fisherman's child, compared to the lives of these scribes destined to work on the great gospel book of St Columba?* But every time I looked at the child, Bethoc, the phrase 'a life for a life' sang in my mind.

I said nothing, however. I waited until the three makeshift coffins were hurriedly put together, until the three graves were dug beside the little stone church on the hillside. I waited until after the burial service – I even made all my farewells to the fisherman's family. Then I walked beside Father Brendan down to the little pier, where a boat waited to take us across the short stretch of water to Iona.

'Father,' I began nervously, 'I have made up my mind. I don't want to go to Iona; I don't want to be a priest. I want to go back to Drumshee. I should never have left it. My father will need me at the forge – he'll see that, once he gets over the sorrow of Conan's death.'

I stopped there. Father Brendan had turned to face me, and I thought he was going to answer; but, so suddenly that I was taken completely off guard, he raised his fist and knocked me to the ground. Before I could gather my wits, he threw the whole weight of his body on me, holding me prisoner. I struggled wildly – I thought he had gone mad – but I was still weak and dizzy from the blow to my head, and he was stronger than I would have thought possible. With one hand he loosened his belt, tied my ankles together and passed the belt around my wrists, pulling the knots cruelly tight. Then he snatched off the linen cloth that he wore around his neck to prevent the sun from burning him, and stuffed it into my mouth.

'Now listen to me, Columba,' he hissed in my ear.

'You are mine. I taught you everything you know – you would be nothing without me. I own you, you are my slave; I can do anything I wish with you. You're coming to Iona with me. I promised God to bring four scribes to work on the great gospel of St Columba. You have lost the lives of three of those scribes; you must take their places. If you try to escape, I'll have you brought back and killed as a runaway slave.'

Then, without another glance at me, he stood up, went to the edge of the water and scooped up a handful of foam from the sea. He smeared it over my face. I tried to say something, but the cloth in my mouth gagged me; all I could do was groan. I saw him grin in satisfaction. Then he cupped his hands around his mouth.

'Help!' he shouted, and I heard the sound of the two boatmen's feet pounding up the little pathway from the pier.

'What's the matter, Father?' shouted one of them. They came to a halt, staring down at me. I knew how I must look to them. The sea-froth over my face would make it look as if I foamed at the mouth.

'The boy has had a fit,' said Father Brendan calmly. 'He's prone to the falling sickness. He'll be himself again in an hour or two. I've put my neckcloth in his mouth to stop him from biting his tongue. Lift him into the boat.'

'Should we wait until he's himself again?' said the other boatman hesitantly. 'He might upset the boat. I've seen a man with the falling sickness, and when he was in a fit he had the strength of ten.'

'No,' said Father Brendan authoritatively. 'I know this boy. The worst is over. We'll leave him bound and leave the gag in his mouth until we reach Iona. If he struggles, one of you can easily subdue him with the handle of the oar.'

After that I knew it would be pointless to struggle, impossible to get the boatmen to release me. Even if somehow I freed myself, as good Christians they would believe the priest, not me. Who was to say whether I was a slave boy or not? Who would believe that I had come of my own free will? I wasn't a monk – that was plain to see: the three young monks who had drowned, and Father Brendan himself, all had the fronts of their heads shaven in the monk's tonsure, but my fair hair hung forward in a fringe. It was believable that I might be a slave. I would wait until I got to Iona, I thought, and then see whether I could get the abbot to believe me.

I lay still, therefore, and made no move while they carried me down the pier and placed me in the bottom of their coracle. The day was fine, the air was still and the sea seemed calm.

'Is that where you're going to land us?' asked Father Brendan, pointing. 'Is that the bay where our blessed St Columba landed?'

'It is indeed, Father. They say he buried his coracle there on the beach so he'd never be tempted to go back to Ireland. Have you heard that story?'

'Yes,' said Father Brendan, but he said no more, and the boatmen did not speak again until, as I judged, we were more than halfway across. Then a bell sounded from the island ahead.

'They'll be in church when you arrive, Father,' said one of the boatmen. 'There'll be no one left to greet you.'

'We'll carry the young fellow up the hill for you,' said the other. 'We could probably untie him now; he seems quiet enough.'

'No,' said Father Brendan. 'We'll leave him as he is.'

When we arrived, he himself held my shoulders to lift me out of the boat, while one of the boatmen took my knees and the other held the boat steady. 'Put him here on the sand,' said Father Brendan, and I lay there looking up at them. I tried to appeal to the boatmen with my eyes, but they looked away, embarrassed.

'Leave us now,' said Father Brendan. 'I will sit here and pray, and when the time is right I'll untie him.'

So they left – how could I expect anything else from them? As soon as the sound of the oars grew faint, Father Brendan leaned over and began to talk to me.

'I've been to Iona several times,' he said quietly. 'The last time I left, I thought I would never see the blessed island again. Then, two years ago, a travelling monk came to Clogher and told us how the monks on Iona were making a great gospel book to celebrate the life of St Columba. He told us that they would need help if the book was to be finished by 797, the two-hundredth anniversary of St Columba's death. Now there's only one year left. I trained those young monks, and they're a sad loss; they were competent workers. But you – you are different; you are an artist. You could do great work on this book for the glory of God. When men look at this book in the future, they will marvel at it. Why do you want to go back to Drumshee? No one wants you there. Why should you want to be a blacksmith? You'll be able to work on this great book, and that is something you will remember all your life.'

Leaning over, he plucked the linen cloth from my mouth. I spat out loose fibres and longed for a drink, but I said nothing. It was no use shouting; the boatmen had gone too far, and in any case they would believe him, not me.

'Listen to me,' continued Father Brendan. 'I'll make a bargain with you. You may take the tonsure and become a monk here, or you may be my slave. It's up to you what I tell the abbot.'

'I'll never become a monk,' I said sullenly. A slave would be better, I thought. I didn't want to take vows that I knew I wouldn't keep. I was a strong swimmer; I would be able to escape. The distance from Iona to Mull wasn't great – less than a mile, I reckoned; I had often swum that distance across Liscannor Bay.

'Then you'll be my slave,' he replied firmly.

'If I become your slave, will there be an end to my slavery?' I asked bitterly.

Father Brendan nodded. 'Yes,' he said. 'On the day when the great gospel book of St Columba is finished – on that blessed day, you will go free. Remember, though: there will be no escape before that day.'

So he brought me up the hill, my legs untied but my hands still bound. The monks were coming out of a little church set within a circular wall. It looked just like the settlement at Clogher: the little church, the monks' cells, the round tower, all dotted around the green enclosed circle. The thought of Clogher brought a lump of homesickness to my throat. Father Brendan left me by the gate while he crossed the grass to speak with a man who seemed to be the abbot. I avoided the curious glances of the monks and looked around. Iona wasn't a big island – about three miles long and a mile wide, Bethoc's father had told me. The land was good, he had said: the lime of the seashells sweetened the fields where the sheep grazed, and I could see that the grass was intensely green. Some corn still waved in the late-August sunshine, though many of the fields had already been harvested and in the distance I could hear the hum of grinding from a little mill, its wheel turned by the falling water of a small stream.

'This is the boy, Abbot,' said Father Brendan, coming back to the gate. 'You can see how sullen he looks,' he added, in a lower voice. 'I think that it had better be as I've recommended. We can always be more lenient later on, if he seems to be well-intentioned.'

'I don't like it,' said the abbot, looking at me. He was a small round man with a sweet face and a gentle voice. 'If the boy is lettered, surely we should not be treating him like this.'

Father Brendan said nothing; he just stood there,

with his cold grey eyes fixed on the abbot and his thin, bloodless lips compressed into a hard line.

The abbot sighed. 'Very well, then,' he said sadly. 'It shall be as you wish; he is your property, and under God you have responsibility for him.'

'Come,' said Father Brendan, seizing me by the arm and leading me down the hill towards the sea.

I knew where we were going before I saw the building. I knew that smell so well, that smell of fire. I knew the sounds, too: the noisy puffing of the bellows, the clanging of iron, the hiss of hot metal when water was thrown over it. For a moment I was puzzled. Had Father Brendan changed his mind about setting me to work on the gospel book? Was he going to put me to work in a forge instead?

A moment later I knew the truth.

'Shackle him,' said Father Brendan to the three men at the forge. 'The abbot bids it.'

Before I could do anything except cry out in protest, two of the men had seized me, and the third picked up a heavy, short length of chain and shackled my legs together. I could move by shuffling one leg in front of the other, but I could not run and I could not swim. There would be no escape for me. I was a prisoner on Iona.

Chapter 13

The year passed. For a while I thought of doing nothing, of refusing to take the quill in my hand, but that mood passed quickly. Father Brendan was a man of his word: as soon as the gospel book of St Columba was finished he would release me – I would be of no use to him then. I fancied that he himself missed Ireland. From time to time I saw him standing on a rock in the Bay of the Coracle, where we had landed and where, more than two hundred years ago, St Columba had come to shore. His face was always turned south, towards Ireland, and there was always a look of great longing on his face. A strange man, I thought – not a bad man underneath, but a man driven by some demons within him; a man who had to go through with a task, no matter what pain it caused him or those around him.

So I worked and he worked. Side by side, day after day, we worked on the gospel book. As we sat there, with no noise but the sound of the quills on the vellum, I could forget my shackled legs; I felt myself his equal.

'You do this,' he said to me, passing me a new sheet of vellum, one day in the late summer after I had been on Iona for about a year. 'I was going to start the Gospel of St John today, but your artistry is greater than mine.'

I hesitated. 'Would it not be best for you to do it?' I asked. 'Surely this is the most important page to be done?'

'No,' he said. 'You have been taught by me; there is no difference between us. Except . . .' He stopped, and I could sense the struggle within him; but, though harsh, he was honest. 'Except that you are an artist and I am but a craftsman. I copy; you create.'

And he got up and left the little scriptorium where we worked. For a moment I almost felt sorry for him, but this vanished in the excitement of the task ahead of me. I was alone that day – the other monks from the Iona community who normally worked with us had gone fishing. I got up and moved around the little hut, collecting what I needed. First I took a lump of lapis lazuli, that intensely blue stone from the east. With the mortar and pestle, I ground the stone carefully; when it was as fine as dust, I mixed the powder with white of egg. Now I had a cow-horn of blue ink. I made green ink from verdigris, the green powder that forms on copper when it is left out in the rain; I made a brilliant red ink from vermilion, yellow from sulphur, black from soot, each carefully mixed with egg-white. Carefully, one by one, I filled the hollow shells of cow-horns with my inks.

I was ready to start, but for a moment I stared out of the door of the scriptorium with eyes that were filled with tears. Making these inks had brought back memories of my childhood at Drumshee, down in the underground room mixing my inks in my little pots with Sorcha by my side, laughing, exclaiming, praising, sharing in my triumphs. I wondered whether I would ever see her again – and, if I did, whether she would walk away from me as she had that morning after we buried Conan. I blotted the tears from my eyes with the back of my wrist, and stroked the soft skin of the vellum to comfort myself.

Then, with a steady hand, I picked up my quill and dipped it into the horn of black ink. St John was my favourite saint; I drew him with Jarlath's gentle face. Then my quill curved and spiralled over the page: the head of an animal, the beak of a bird, the sinuous coils of a snake all emerged from the flowing nib. Hours passed. I began to fill the shapes with colour; blues and reds and yellows and greens came to my hand without hesitation. Father Brendan came

127

back, and he handed me the quills I needed: a swan's feather for the noble strokes of bold red, a swallow's wing-feather for the dot of yellow in the bird's eye, a raven's iridescent feather for the verdigris spirals.

'Rest now,' he said at last. 'The light is fading; go to your cell and sleep. You have done well today. In years to come, men will speak of this page.'

He placed his hand on my shoulder, but I shuffled away from him without a word. I could never forget what he had done to me – that he had shackled me like a runaway beast from the fields, kept me from my home, from my love. Once again I thought of Sorcha, her sad pale face with swollen eyes. I wished I could be near her – not to demand her love, but simply to care for her, to cook her food, to chop wood for her fire.

I went to my cell, but I could not sleep. The wind had come up. Abbot Bresal had been right when he had sent all the other monks fishing that day: no boat would be able to set out to sea for the next week. The storms of the autumn had come, and with them the high tides of that quarter of the year. From my cell on top of the hill I could hear the waves thundering against the cliffs in the Bay of the Coracle. Towards dawn I slept heavily for an hour or so, my dreams troubled by the green coils of snakes spiralling around my legs, shackling them together.

I woke with a start when the bell tolled for the dawn service. My head was heavy with sleep and my eyes stung with the tears I had shed. I slipped out of my cell, but I didn't join the column of monks filing into the church. I turned my face towards the southwesterly wind that still blew strongly and made my way down to the Bay of the Coracle.

For a moment I thought I had taken the wrong way. Everything looked different. The tide had gone right out, and I hardly recognised the beach. The storm had made great changes: the white sand was strewn with boulders hacked from the cliff above, and much sand had been swept away, exposing stretches of water-worn pebbles. A wooden shape stuck up from the middle of the beach – perhaps part of a ship that had been lost. As quickly as my shackled legs would allow, I crossed the sand and stood looking down at the wood.

It was indeed the prow of a boat – perhaps more than the prow: there was no broken edge to be seen. Quickly I dug at the soft powdery sand, scraping it away with my hands. There seemed to be a whole boat underneath. It was the same sort of coracle as the one in which we had left Ireland, but the wood was black with age. The frame was covered with leather skins – not carefully sewn like the ones on our boat; Jarlath had taught me to do all things well, and my stitches had been the same size and as small as possible, but these stitches were large and uneven.

Kneeling there on the sand, I remembered Father Brendan's stories about St Columba's arrival at Iona, and I remembered the boatman's words: *They say he buried his coracle there on the beach so he would never be tempted to go back to Ireland . . .*

Could this be the buried coracle of St Columba? Was it possible that a boat could survive in the sand for over two hundred years? I began to dig with my hands, scooping out the sand and piling it beside the boat. Before I finished I was sweating heavily, despite the cool wind, but the discomfort of my body and my aching back was nothing compared to the agony of my mind. Every minute I thought I would surely find the boat was damaged beyond repair; every minute I feared to hear voices above, people who would discover what I was doing and destroy the tiny, feeble flame of hope that had lit itself within me.

But, for the first time in my life, luck was with me. The boat – *surely*, I thought, *it must be St Columba's* – was whole and undamaged. The leather skins that covered it were still doing their original task: none of them had shrunk away from the wooden frame, and they were all still fairly supple. Even the leather sail, on the mast lying in the bottom of the boat, was still soft, with no cracks. *Of course*, I thought: the sea flooded the sands twice every day. The leather had been kept damp the whole time. And perhaps some substance in this powder-fine white sand had helped to preserve it; I knew that such things were possible.

I could get away in this boat. I could get back to Ireland. It had oars lying in the bottom – too many for my needs, but I would keep four, to have a spare pair in case of any mishap. I didn't care how long it took. I would set my course to the south and keep going until I reached the coast of Ireland. Quickly I glanced around; all the monks were in church, I knew, but some curious villager might be watching. No one was in sight, though. The sands, the cliffs and the heaving ocean were all bare of people.

In a frantic hurry, I began to pile the sand back into the boat; I brought more and more sand until the whole boat was covered, hidden. I prayed that no one would come near the rough heap of sand before the tide came in, and that, if they did, they would think it had simply been disturbed by the high wind. Once the boat was covered I went around the beach frantically digging and heaping up the sand in other spots, so that the spot where the boat lay would be less conspicuous. Then slowly I dragged myself, with my shackled legs, up the steep slope of the hill, and went to the kitchen-house for my breakfast.

'You're hungry this morning,' said old Brother Ninian, as I filled my bowl with porridge a second time.

'Yes,' I said. 'I went for a walk before breakfast to clear my head. I slept badly because of the storm.'

Normally I said very little to Brother Ninian, but that morning I wanted to stay in the kitchen-house as long as possible. I noted the shelf where the big water-skins were stored: I would need to take some water with me, I knew. I could fill one of them with water from the stream. I should take food, too, if possible – though I felt that, if only I could get back to Drumshee, I would not need food on the way. Still, I would need energy if a lack of wind forced me to row. My eyes went to a row of big baskets made of plaited rushes. They seemed to be full of bread.

'You bake great bread,' I said. 'Do you bake it every day?'

'Most days,' Brother Ninian said, smiling happily at my compliment. 'I have enough at the moment, so I'll bake hardcake today. The mill will be running fast after all the rain last night; I'll use up some of the extra flour on hardcake, and then I can put it aside for the next time anyone goes on a journey.'

I nodded. This was good news. Hardcake lasted for weeks; it would be ideal for my voyage. My eyes wandered around the room.

'You've made plenty of cheese, too,' I said.

'At this time of year the cows give more milk than we can drink, so I use up the rest making cheese; soon the cows will go dry, and we'll have the cheese instead of milk. Listen – there are the monks coming from the church. You'd better slip out before Father Brendan catches you; if he sees you here, he'll know you haven't been to morning prayers.'

I smiled at him and slipped out the back door. It had no lock, I noticed.

But I had one more thing to do before I could make my escape. It would be no good setting off on this journey with my legs shackled. The monks were busy at breakfast; Father Brendan wouldn't look for me for some time yet. Stumbling in my eagerness, I made my way back down the hill towards the forge. Perhaps it, like the kitchen-house, was left open at night . . .

That was probably too much to hope for, though; luck couldn't go my way all through that day. The blacksmith and his men were already at work, and on the door of the forge was a large, heavy iron lock. There was no hope that I would be able to break it open and steal a file to cut the shackles from my legs. I sat on a rock in front of the forge, wretched and weary and more homesick than ever.

The men greeted me in subdued tones and then went on with their work. I could feel that they were uneasy with me; from time to time, I saw them casting sidelong glances at me and then at each other. I couldn't think of anything to say to them. All I could think of was my father, working at his forge with no son to help him. Tears welled up in my eyes.

'It's a shame,' I heard one of the men mutter.

'He's only a boy,' said another. 'He's no older than my Neil. I'd like to see anyone do that to him!'

'Cheer up, lad,' said the blacksmith. 'One of these days we'll be filing those shackles off your legs. I heard Abbot Bresal talking about it to Father Brendan the other day, and Father Brendan said he'd consider it when winter comes. You'll only have to put up with them for another few months – or less, if the abbot has his way.'

'It's not that,' I muttered. 'I was just feeling homesick. My father's a blacksmith, and I was thinking about how he's been left with no one to help him – my brother is dead.'

'A blacksmith! Well, I never knew that. I thought you were just a scholar.'

The blacksmith said no more for a while; but from time to time, as he worked, I heard low, muttered words between the blows of his hammer. 'A blacksmith . . . No son left to work with him . . . God help him.'

After a while, he shouted: 'Duncan and Malcolm, the two of you go and fetch the old grey plough-horse. He needs new shoes. We'll do that this morning.'

The men looked surprised, and I was surprised too: it wouldn't take two men to fetch that quiet old horse. However, they went off without question, and I heard their voices growing fainter as they climbed the hill. They were talking about the dreaded Norsemen – Vikings, people called them – who had been raiding islands to the north, stealing and killing and burning all before them. I had heard the monks speak of these Vikings, too: another abbey had been raided, sacred books destroyed, communion cups stolen.

The blacksmith had ceased work and was also listening to the men's chatter. When we could no longer hear them, he went quickly to a shelf in the forge and came back with a small, sharp file in his hand. I gasped.

'Put that in your pouch, Columba,' he whispered.

'Tell no one, show it to no one. Only use it when the time is right – and never betray me.'

'I'll never forget what you've done,' I said earnestly, hastily opening the drawstring of my pouch and concealing the file inside.

He patted me on the shoulder. 'Give my greetings to my brother blacksmith in Ireland,' he said. 'Now go. Say nothing, tell no one your plans – but remember, the turf boat from the mainland will be here in a fortnight's time. You might be able to hide in that and get to the mainland. From there, a lad like you might be able to work his passage back to Ireland.'

That was another possibility. I pondered it as I dragged my way back up the steep path. It might be safer: St Columba's boat might not be seaworthy; it might spring a leak a few miles out to sea. On the other hand, the men on the turf boat might discover me instantly and hand me back to Father Brendan – and, even if I did reach the mainland, I would have no one to help me, and I might not find a way to get back to Ireland. No, I decided: I would prefer to go in St Columba's boat.

Chapter 14

All that day, as my hand worked on the gospel book, my mind worked on my plan to escape. I wouldn't be able to go for a few days yet, until the heavy seas calmed down. I would use that time to test the boat, I decided. I would dig it up that night and drag it into one of the deep caves under the cliff. I knew one that would be ideal; when the tide rose, the sea rushed in and filled it, so I would be able to test the seaworthiness of my boat. The tide would come in overnight, and sand would fill the hole the boat would leave on the beach.

Saturday, I thought, changing my quill for a tiny brush made from pine-marten fur; Saturday would be the best night to go. At midnight the tide would be half in, and all the monks would be in the church – they had an extra-long service that night. I would have everything ready, and as soon as the bell stopped ringing I would go; I would be well out to sea before they discovered my absence.

It was Wednesday: I had three nights to test my boat, stock it with water and food and make all ready for my journey. Secretly, over those three days, I kept touching the small, sharp file in my pouch. I had an almost overwhelming desire to remove the shackles from my ankles; only the thoughts of Sorcha and of Drumshee made me resist. Everything would have to be done at the right moment if this escape was to succeed – and the right moment to remove my shackles was not till midnight on Saturday.

Saturday night was cold and still, with a smell of frost in the air. When the church bell went at midnight, I sat up in my bed and filed the shackles from my ankles. I blessed the kindly blacksmith: the file was sharp enough for a man to shave his beard with, and after only a few minutes' work I was free. I left the chain on the floor beside my bed, but halfway down the cliff I turned back, gathered it up and carried it with me. I would throw it in the sea, I decided; it would be shameful of me to risk letting my friend the blacksmith be blamed for my escape.

If I had not done that – if I had not gone back again – perhaps I would have escaped without seeing what I saw, perhaps I would have escaped unaccompanied; but I can't bring myself to wish that things had been different. If they had, a thing of great beauty would have been lost forever, perhaps even destroyed.

I went down the hill and entered my cave. I had brought no lantern, and I needed none. The moon and the stars lit my path; they even penetrated into the dark cave where my little boat rocked on the black water. I threw my shackles and chain into the bottom of the boat. The food and water I had taken the night before were already there. Everything was ready for the journey.

I was not alone, though, on that silent beach at midnight. There on the fine powdery sand, where St Columba's boat had lain buried for over two hundred years, were two long ships – much longer than any ship I had ever seen. They were built differently, too: instead of wooden frames covered with leather, these ships seemed to be made of overlapping planks of wood, with narrow, upward-jutting prows.

There were men in them – men with great helmets and large swords that would take two hands to wield. They were lowering their sails, stowing their oars and making their ships safe on the sand. I could hear their lowered voices, but I couldn't understand what they said. But I had no need to know what they were saying in order to know that they were Norsemen, Vikings, and they were going to attack Iona.

At the time it felt as if my struggle with myself was endless, but it could only have lasted less than a minute. I had received many kindnesses during my time at Iona; I could not leave the monks to be murdered in their church as a fox murders helpless hens roosting in their house. In a moment I was running back up the cliff path, towards the enclosure.

The bell-rope hung outside the round tower. I pulled it violently, splintering the frosty air with the bell's clamour, then ran to the church. All was silent within; the monks turned towards the door, wondering who had rung the bell.

'Vikings!' I screamed. 'Save yourselves!'

I turned and ran back down the cliff path. I wasn't going to miss my chance of escape. There were over a hundred and fifty monks in the community, as well as the workers; they could fight the Vikings themselves. Whether I went or stayed would make little difference to the outcome.

Already the invaders had started to climb the path at the right-hand side of the beach. The path to my cave was at the other side of the beach, and it was small and narrow and heavily screened by gorse bushes; I was sure the Vikings wouldn't notice me.

But when I was about halfway down the cliff I heard someone behind me. There were heavy footsteps, laboured breathing and the rolling of a few stones kicked by flying feet. I took no notice, though. I didn't care who was behind me; I was determined to escape. I could wait no longer. Even if the Vikings were driven off, I wouldn't be missed for days – perhaps never; the monks might assume that I had been killed, or captured by the Vikings.

Quickly I waded into the cave. The tide was at just the right level; my boat rocked gently, the food and water safe in the bottom. I tugged at it gently and dragged it out to the edge of the sea.

'Columba,' said a voice from behind me, and I froze with terror. 'Columba, I'm going with you.'

Anger replaced fear. I knew that voice. It was Father Brendan – the man who had tricked me, who had cheated me, who had shackled me and kept me from my home and from my love. Swiftly I pulled the heavy chain from the bottom of the boat and swung it up. There was murder in my mind, and I would have killed him if he had not spoken quickly.

'Columba,' he said, 'I have the gospel book here with me, in my satchel. We can't leave it for the Vikings to destroy.'

I hesitated. I knew that the Vikings stole what was useful and valuable to them; what they did not want, they destroyed. They would burn the sacred book. All my work, that beautiful page at the beginning of St John's Gospel, would never be seen again.

'Get in,' I said through gritted teeth.

I held the boat steady while he pulled up his long brown tunic, waded into the sea, then climbed in and placed the leather satchel in the bottom of the boat. The weight rocked the boat, which surprised me. *He must have something else in there*, I thought; *the book couldn't be as heavy as that.* He took a length of oiled sealskin from under his arm and wrapped it around the satchel, tucking its ends underneath so that no drop of water could get to the precious book, then tied it with cord.

'Row,' I said impatiently. 'If you value anything in this boat, row as you've never rowed before.'

He wasn't much good; I would have made better progress on my own in the boat. I wished I were ruthless enough to knock the life out of him with my iron shackles, but it wasn't in me to do it. However, I took an evil delight in hearing the breath rasp in his throat as we made our way against the incoming tide.

'Can't we put up the sail?' he gasped after about twenty minutes.

'Not until we're out of sight of Iona,' I told him. 'And not even then, if we hear the Vikings take to sea.'

But there was little chance of the Vikings coming back to their longships for a while yet, I thought. Sound travelled well in the clear, cold air, and I could hear the noises of battle raging on the hill of Iona. The hundred and fifty monks would fight well, and so would their servants and workmen. My warning had given them time to get their knives and clubs. The Vikings would not have an easy victory.

We rowed on until day dawned and the moon was just a smoky shape in the southwestern sky. The sea was empty except for a few fishing-boats by the coastline of Scotland.

'We can put the sails up now,' I said. 'There's a north wind blowing. If we can keep it to our backs, we'll be in Liscannor by tomorrow.'

'Columba,' Father Brendan began, laying down his pair of oars.

'Keep rowing,' I interrupted. 'Don't stop. You keep the boat steady while I raise the sail.'

It gave me a savage pleasure to order him about. For a moment he seemed about to argue, but then, silently, he began to row again. He handled the oars awkwardly. I guessed that his hands were beginning to blister, but I had no mercy on him.

I kept him rowing for about ten minutes longer than was needed, but then I began to pity him. He had done me terrible injury – by accusing me of Conan's death he had destroyed any trace of feeling that my father and mother had ever had for me, he had shamed me by putting shackles on my legs as if I were a criminal; but I couldn't forget how he had taught me to read and write, and to make books of great beauty.

'You can stop,' I told him. 'The wind's strong enough now. We can both take a rest.'

He dropped the oars thankfully. He was exhausted; I could hear his breath sobbing in his breast, and his hands trembled like those of a man in a high fever. It wasn't for my sake that he had exerted every muscle in his body, of course – and, to give him his due, nor had it been to save his own skin. I knew him well by now. It had all been to save the gospel book of St Columba.

'Sleep,' I said roughly. 'One man can manage the sails. I'll wake you when I need you.'

Without a word he stretched himself in the bottom of the boat, hardly bothering to shift the two pairs of oars out of his way. In a moment he was asleep.

He slept for the whole day. Although the boat plunged and bucked with the gusts of wind forcing it through the rough waves, Father Brendan never moved. Towards nightfall the wind dropped, though there was still enough to keep the boat moving. This was my chance to sleep.

'Father Brendan,' I called. 'Can you manage the boat for a few hours while I rest?'

He woke slowly, dazed. Slowly he reached out and touched the leather satchel, still safely wrapped in its oiled sealskin.

'All's well?' he asked.

I nodded. 'We should be passing Donegal by morning. We're making good time.'

'Columba,' he said. Then he paused, like a man making sure all his arguments are properly marshalled before he speaks. *He's going to try to persuade me into doing something I don't want to do*, I thought. I bent down and touched the iron shackles still lying in the bottom of the boat, to remind myself, to make sure I wouldn't give in.

'Columba,' Father Brendan continued solemnly, 'I don't wish to go back to Liscannor. I don't wish to go back to Clogher. I want you to sail this boat down the east coast of Ireland, not the west. We must take the sacred gospel book to St Columba's own monastery at Kells. There it must stay, in the care of the monks there. Kells is under the protection of the King of Armagh. Clogher is too poor and too unimportant to house this magnificent book.'

For a moment I hesitated. I was so used to doing what he ordered. And he was right, of course: Kells would be the best place for the book. I remembered the care I had put into the opening page of St John's Gospel, the magnificent colours . . . But then I thought of Sorcha's eyes, the same brilliant blue as the lapis lazuli, and her gentle face; and I knew the living girl was more important to me than any book.

'No,' I said harshly. 'We're going to Liscannor. You can take the book to Kells by road afterwards, if you want. I'm going back to Drumshee where I belong.'

He knew better than to argue with me. I had changed, hardened. He was getting old; I was just coming to my full strength. If it became necessary, I would beat him to death with those iron shackles that he had ordered to be placed around my ankles. He lifted the well-wrapped leather satchel onto his knees and turned away from me. I could see his lips moving in prayer.

And so, in silence, we made our way down the west coast of Ireland. We passed Donegal, Sligo, Mayo; Galway was ahead, and beyond it the little port of Liscannor. I remember how supremely happy I felt. That year in Iona had added inches to my height, strength to my legs and arms, and years of maturity and confidence to my spirit. I think it was on the day when Father Brendan acknowledged that I was the superior artist, when he gave me the first page of the Gospel of St John to do, that confidence came to me.

I looked at him with compassion. The golden half-circle of Liscannor Bay was·in sight, but his face was grey and drawn as he hugged the leather satchel to him.

'We'll be there soon,' I said gently. 'Look, there's Liscannor. You'll be able to rest at Clogher for a while and then get a horse to carry you to Kells. Some of the other monks will go with you. The journey won't take more than a few days.'

He shook his head wordlessly. I forgot him and went back to my own thoughts.

I thought about Conan, and I found I could think of him without bitterness or guilt. Father Brendan had once shown me a wonderful jewel green as the ocean. 'This gem should be worth a king's ransom,' he had said, 'but in its depths it holds a fatal flaw. This is why we can grind it up to make our ink.' Conan had been like that jewel, I thought: brilliant, fascinating, beautiful, bringing joy to all who knew him – but deep inside him he had held the fatal flaw that led him to his terrible treachery that midnight.

I could understand and forgive him, and I could move on to lead my own life.

I would go back to Drumshee, I thought. I would go to my father and mother, and take them both in my arms. My mother would love me now – I was sure of that. It was my brother's death that had scarred her and driven all her love towards Conan; but now I was her only son. And then, my happy thoughts went on, I would go over to Mount Callan. I would meet Sorcha; soon we would be betrothed, and in a few years I would have sons and daughters of my own, and each of them would be loved as Jarlath and Dervilla had loved us both . . . I was like a man drunk with happiness, on that late-summer day. The blue sky was above me, the blue sea beneath me, and the sands of the bay were a bright gold.

I had forgotten, of course, what I should have been keeping in mind at that moment. I had forgotten all the careful instructions Jarlath had given me when, so long ago, he had taught me to swim. I had forgotten the river that made a treacherous, sucking current on the north side of Liscannor Bay; and I had forgotten the great waves that can suddenly arise even on the calmest of days.

We were well into the bay. In my excitement, I had not aimed for the centre of the bay but was coming in on the nearest side, the north side. The current seized the little boat and spun it around – and then, while I was lowering the sail, the freak wave came. Out of a still sea it moved swiftly towards shore, like a monster appearing from the depths of the sea. It seemed as tall as Mount Callan and its sides were smooth as glass.

'Take the oars!' I screamed to Father Brendan, but he sat like a man stunned, still clutching the leather satchel. He would probably have been of little use, anyway. The next second the wave picked us up and tossed us in the air, the boat turned over and I was struggling in the sea.

It was all over in a moment: the wave passed on and hit the rocks with a thunderous crash, and then suddenly the sea was calm again. I knew the danger, though. Suddenly my mind had woken up, and I remembered how Jarlath had shown me the path of the River Cullenagh, where the sinking sands sucked beneath the sea. To head straight for the shore would be madness – I would be pulled under by the current from the river – so I struck out strongly towards the middle of the bay. I had only a few moments to get well away before the wave ebbed back out and dragged me into the path of the dangerous river current, but that sense of confidence was still strong in me and I remember no feeling of fear. There were men on the shore: I heard them shout, saw them pull off cloaks and tunics and run into the sea on the south side of the bay.

Sorcha! I thought, and that was the last thing I remember.

Chapter 8

'Lapis lazuli,' I thought – or did I say it sleepily? The blue eyes above me looked startled. I moved, and something – an iron bedstead – creaked beneath me. I blinked. The eyes were still there, and they were Sorcha's eyes. But her hair, her beautiful golden hair? The woman bending over me had her head wrapped in linen, a white veil flowing over her shoulders.

'He's awake,' said another voice.

Sorcha moved aside. Her place was taken by another face: grey eyes, lined face, head wrapped in snowy white, black veil flowing.

'Lie still,' said the second voice. 'You're at the convent at Kilshanny. We'll care for you. You were rescued from the sea, but you're badly bruised and you hit your head on the rocks.'

Father Brendan, I thought, but I was too sick of heart to inquire about him. Sorcha, a nun – lost to me forever . . . *Truly*, I thought, *I am the devil's child.* She was coming to my bedside again, those blue eyes filled with tears – tears of joy, it seemed – but I wouldn't look at her. I turned my head away and

151

buried my face in the soft pillow.

'Leave me,' I said, and my voice was rough and choked with tears. 'Leave me. I would sleep now.'

I heard footsteps crossing the floor and the door shutting – but it was only one set of footsteps, and I could still hear small movements in the room. I stole a glance, but it was the elderly woman who had remained, not Sorcha. She had gone. There would have been no point in her remaining, I thought bitterly. She was a nun now. She had not been able to put Conan from her mind; for her, life was not worth living without him, and so she had given her life to God. I was nothing to her.

There was a tap at the door. The elderly nun crossed over swiftly and held a short whispered conversation. Then she came back and stood beside my bed.

'Eanna the fisherman is here,' she said. 'Do you feel strong enough to talk to him? He was the one who pulled you from the sea.'

For a moment I thought of pretending to be asleep, but shame overcame me and I turned over. I fixed a smile on my frozen lips and did my best to thank him. He brushed the thanks aside.

'I only came to tell you that the body came ashore,' he said.

My head was still heavy from its battering against the rocks, but slowly I began to realise what he meant.

'Father Brendan? He drowned?' I asked. An odd feeling of loss came over me. I was still weak, I suppose. I closed my eyes, but warm tears trickled down from beneath the lids.

'Don't blame yourself. You couldn't have saved him,' said Eanna urgently. 'He must have sunk like a stone. He was holding that bundle – it feels like a box of lead; it's a miracle the body came ashore, with that weighting it down. It was washed in by another of those freak waves. We picked it up from the shoreline at low tide.'

'Box?' I said.

'Yes, didn't you know? Inside the bundle there's a box. By the weight of it, I reckon it's made from lead. I haven't looked in it – it's for you to open it, but Mother Abbess thought you wouldn't want to be bothered with it yet.'

'I'd like to see it, Mother Abbess,' I said humbly to the old nun. 'I think it's the gospel book of St Columba.'

She put a cool, dry hand on my forehead for a moment and then nodded to the fisherman. He left the room with alacrity, like a man who wants to hand over a responsibility as soon as possible.

When Eanna returned with the box he was followed by about ten other nuns, all full of curiosity to see the gospel book. They all looked so alike, with their linen-wrapped heads and their flowing black veils, that I had to look closely from face to face to be sure that Sorcha wasn't there. It didn't matter, anyway, I told myself. She had been Conan's; now she was God's. She never had been – and never would be – mine.

Eanna placed the bundle on a low table near my bed. The nuns crowded around eagerly. I was too weak to move, but he unwrapped the sodden sealskins, dropping them to the floor, and took out the leather satchel.

'It's hardly wet,' whispered the abbess, making the sign of the cross. 'God has preserved it.' The other nuns huddled nearer, but still there was no sign of Sorcha.

'Here's the box,' said Eanna. 'I was right – it's made of lead.'

He brought it over to my bedside and put it into my hands so I could feel the weight of it. *It must have been made especially for the gospel book*, I thought. The size was right; and on the lid was the interlacing pattern of spirals that I had drawn again and again on the manuscript.

'Open it,' I said.

He obeyed.

'It's perfect,' he said, holding up the beautiful book. 'Not a drop of water got through to it.'

The abbess and her nuns fell to their knees and gave thanks to God, but I wasn't listening. The book had been preserved, and I was glad of that; but now I had to keep faith with Father Brendan.

'Eanna,' I said, 'could you take the satchel and the book to Clogher? Tell the monks that the one wish of Father Brendan's was that the gospel book of St Columba should be taken to St Columba's monastery at Kells. They'll see to it.'

Then I closed my eyes. I could hear the abbess hushing the young nuns and ordering them out; at the doorway she whispered to Eanna, 'He's overtired. He'll be recovered in a few days, though; he's a strong young man.'

She was right. In a few days I was myself again. I was eager to get back to Drumshee – perhaps one part of my dream of happiness, at least, might come true. I saw Sorcha only once during that time, but I turned my head away and didn't acknowledge the half-smile she gave me. There was no point in looking at her, in greeting her. She was forbidden fruit. She was God's, not mine. She left the room at once; I heard the abbess call, 'Sister Sorcha,' after her, but she made no reply and did not return. After that I saw no more of her.

The day was fine and sunny when I set out on the six-mile walk from Kilshanny to Drumshee. The abbess offered me a mule, but I refused. I suppose, deep within myself, some instinct told me to enjoy my dream of finding a mother and a father for a little longer, to enjoy it until reality crept in.

No smoke came from the forge. That was the first thing I noticed as I went up the lane towards Drumshee. There were signs of life, though: I could hear my uncle Aidan bellowing at a cow in the Rough Field, and a high, clear boy's voice replying. I went towards them, crossing the field and the little lane that led to the bog.

'It's not yourself, Columba!' said Aidan. He looked as if I had been away for ten years, not just one. 'God bless you, you've grown – I'd never have known you. Look at the cut of you! Look at those shoulders! You're a big man now.'

'I've grown, too – haven't I, Father?' demanded my cousin Michael. Aidan smiled absently at the child, but I could sense that he was uneasy. For a moment he turned back to the cows; but then I saw his head nod, as if he had made up his mind.

'I have something to tell you, lad,' he said bluntly. 'It's no good holding it back. It will never make easy telling, but you'll have to know it, and better sooner than later. You have lost your father and your mother. Your mother died shortly after Conan's death – of a broken heart, they say – and your father . . .' He hesitated for a moment. 'Well, you know your father was too fond of the drink. He had a bit too much taken one day at Coad Fair, a few months ago, and he got into a fight – something about Conan, it was. He got a bad blow to the head. He lasted a few days, but in the end he died. We buried them both at Clogher.'

So that was the end of that dream. My uncle was kind to me, showed me the forge; the house had been kept for me, a fire was lit there regularly. I could take over the forge immediately. No other blacksmith had come to live in the area. I was as welcome as the sun at hay-making time. Neither he nor my aunt could do enough for me. And yet, and yet . . .

I think no lonelier, sadder young man went to bed that night in all of Ireland. I almost wished I were back on Iona, dragging my shackled feet around the island.

Still, I did sleep, eventually. In fact, it was almost dawn when I woke. The sun hit my face with a shaft of light, and that light illuminated my mind.

The abbess had called her 'Sister Sorcha'. All the other nuns had saints' names — Sister Anne, Sister Mary, Sister Martha, Sister Ursula — but Sorcha wasn't a saint's name. She couldn't be a full nun without a saint's name.

And there was something else. All the other nuns, young and old, had worn black veils; but Sorcha had worn a white one. She wasn't a full nun. She hadn't taken all her vows. She was what they called a postulant: she was there to make up her mind, to try out her vocation. She was still free to leave.

In a moment I was out of bed. The first rays of sunshine were coming across the hills as I dashed to the well, sluiced down my face and head and dragged a comb through my hair. Then, snatching an oat-cake from the plate my aunt had left out the night before, I was off, running down the steep lane from Drumshee.

I would gamble for my last chance of happiness.

epilogue

It was all such a long time ago. I look back and remember Sorcha with her corn-coloured hair . . . Now it's grey, and I love her no less dearly.

The forge is busy these days. I no longer work at it myself, but my two sons and my four grandsons are busy hammering and forging. From where I sit, writing this account, I can hear the hiss of hot metal striking the water, the clang of the hammer and the roar of fire.

That fire in the forge has never gone out since that day in the late summer of the year 797 – the year when Iona was attacked by the Vikings; the year when Sorcha told me, in the convent garden, that she had made no vows. She told me something else that day, also. She told me that, only a few months after I had gone, she had realised that she loved me every bit as much as she had ever loved Conan – in a different way, perhaps, but no less dearly. Her love for Conan had been the first passionate love of a young girl; her love for me was the sweet, steady love of a woman for a man who, all her life, had been her dearest friend.

It was the news that I had become a monk, coming on top of Conan's death, that had driven her into entering the convent herself.

We saw the abbess together; she smiled at Sorcha's happy face and blessed us both. I took Sorcha back to her parents' house near Mount Callan, and then, when I returned to Drumshee, I set the forge fire roaring. My uncle and aunt laughed to see the size of the fire I had made; my young cousins danced around it with glee; and I was filled with such a rush of excitement that I set straight to beating the iron ore from the lumps of sandstone lying around the forge.

There is little more to write of the story of my life. Sorcha and I were married soon after my return, and we saw our children and our grandchildren grow in strength and happiness. Dervilla came to live with us; and in the warmth and love she received from us, and from our children, she learned to forget the sorrow of Jarlath's death.

As for the gospel book of St Columba, it belongs to the monks of Kells now, and no one knows of the part I played in the making of it. I don't care. Only one thing matters: never again was I made to feel that I was the devil's child.